MONSTERS IN THE DARK

At the edge of the ancient ruined city, Morgan Chane faced a dark forest from which came a creature that was manlike but not human. It came toward him and he saw a face that had softly glowing big eyes, no nose at all, and a nauseatingly pretty little mouth. It laughed—a kind of sobbing, shivery laughter.

And suddenly, from behind him, a living weight landed on his back, and smooth cold arms went around his throat, choking him.

All right, thought Chane. *But you haven't caught an Earthman: you've caught a Starwolf.*

He put all his Varnan strength into a great surge to break the grip.

It did not break. And he realized, as he began to gasp for air, that he had finally met something stronger than he was. . . .

D1218464

THE CLOSED WORLDS is the second in Edmond Hamilton's exciting new series of stellar adventures featuring Morgan Chane, the Starwolf. See page 158 for information on the first Starwolf novel, THE WEAPON FROM BEYOND.

The Closed Worlds

Starwolf #2

EDMOND HAMILTON

ACE BOOKS, INC.
1120 Avenue of the Americas
New York, New York 10036

THE CLOSED WORLDS

Cover painting and frontispiece by Jack Gaughan.

THE

CLOSED

WORLDS

I

H<small>E WALKED THE</small> streets of New York, and tried to behave as though he were an Earthman.

If they find out what I really am, I'm dead, thought Morgan Chane.

He looked like an Earthman. Not too tall, with wide shoulders and black hair and a face of dark, hard planes. And he could speak the language well enough. These things were not strange, since his dead parents had been natives of this world. This Earth, which he had never seen until a few days ago.

Don't even think of the fact that you're a Starwolf!

Nobody knew that, except Dilullo. And Dilullo was not going to tell anyone, at least as long as they stayed partners. Which in effect gave Dilullo the power of life and death over him, for death was the swift and certain sentence meted out to a captured Starwolf on nearly every world in the galaxy.

Chane smiled, and thought, *The hell with it.* Danger was living, and if you avoided danger, you were only existing. Anyway, there was small risk of being suspected for what he was, here on a world where he looked just like everyone else. Nobody would even notice him in the crowd.

But they did. People looked at Chane, and looked back at him again. There was a springiness in his step that he could not quite hide. He had been born and reared on Varna, the world of the hated Starwolves, and that was a big and heavy planet. He could adjust his muscles to the lesser gravitation of smaller planets like this Earth, but he could not completely hide the latent strength and speed of his body. And there was something in his dark face, a touch of just faintly inhuman ruthlessness, that made him stand out.

The men looked at him with something of the expression with which they looked at the not-men one occasionally met in this starport quarter. The women looked at him as though they were both scared and attracted. These side-glances began to make Chane a little uncomfortable. He was not afraid of any of these people—a Varnan could break one of them in half—but he didn't want to start anything.

"You've got a genius for finding trouble," Dilullo had told him. "If you get into any here, you're all through as a Merc."

Chane had only shrugged. But the truth was that he didn't want to stop being a Merc. The Mercs . . . the name was short for mercenaries . . . were the second toughest people in space, the hardbitten men, most of them Earthmen, who went out and did all the dirty, dangerous jobs in the galaxy for pay. There were not as tough as the Starwolves, but the Starwolves had thrown him out, and being a Merc was better than anything else open to him.

Chane left the crowded street and went into a tavern. It was pretty crowded too, but most of the customers were men off the starport and their girls, and most of them were too exhilarated to pay attention to Chane. He ordered whisky and drank it, and thought that no matter what Dilullo said it was poor stuff, and then he ordered some more. The din was loud around him but he dropped away from it as he brooded.

He remembered Varna, the place that had always been home to him. The great, harsh, unfriendly, oversized planet which gave its children nothing except the unmatchable strength and speed which its cruelly heavy gravitation bred into their bodies. Even to Chane it had given that, when he had survived being born there. It was as though Varna was a stern mother who told her sons, "I have given you strength and that is all I have to give . . . go forth and take whatever else you want."

And they had gone forth, the sons of Varna! As soon as they learned the way to make starships, from foolish Earthmen who were trying to encourage trade, the Varnans swarmed out to loot the lesser worlds. They were unbeatable in space; no other people could stand the acceleration pressures they could stand. Across the galaxy went the fear of the quick and ruthless ones—the Starwolves!

A smile crossed Chane's brooding face like a ripple upon a dark pool. He could see in memory of the times when their little squadrons would come home, dropping down out of the starry sky toward their grim mother world, the lights, the loot spread out and the laughter, nobody caring much that some had died in the foray: the Varnans striding like conquerors into their cities, their tall bodies splendid in their fine golden-down hair, their high-boned faces proud and their cat-slanted eyes bright.

And he had been one of them. He walked proud with them; he raided the starworlds with them; he lived in the tingle of danger.

It was all gone now; they had driven him out. He would never see Varna again, and here he was, sitting in a stinking room in a dull city on a dull planet.

"Having fun, Chane?"

A hand fell on his shoulder and he looked up into the long, horselike face of Dilullo.

"I'm having fun," said Chane. "I can hardly remember a time when I've had more fun than now."

"That's fine," said the older man, and sat down. "That's just fine. I was afraid you might be pining for some of the fighting and killing and robbing that Varnans call fun. I was so worried about it that I thought I'd keep an eye on you."

Dilullo's bleak, no-colored eyes had an ironic twinkle in them. He turned and ordered a drink.

Chane looked at him, thinking that there were times when he hated Dilullo and that this was one of the times.

Dilullo turned back and then he said, "You know, Chane, you look like a bored tiger sitting there. But the tiger is going to stay bored, and on a short leash. This isn't one of the outworlds, it's Earth; and we're kind of strict here."

"It does seem a bit dull, now that you mention it," said Chane.

Dilullo's drink came and he drank half of it. Then he said, "I thought you might feel that way. So you may be glad to hear that we might just have another job coming up."

Chane looked up quickly. "What job? Where?"

"Don't know yet," said Dilullo. He finished his drink. "But a very big shot in interstellar trade named Ashton wants to see me in the morning. I assume he doesn't want to see a Merc leader without some reason."

"Do you want to take on something so soon?" said Chane. "I mean, we did pretty well on that job for Kharal. I'd suppose you'd want to take a rest."

Dilullo's hard mouth tightened. He looked down at his empty glass, his stubby, strong fingers twirling it around.

"I get my hair cut real short, Chane," he said. "But I can't get it cut short enough to keep the gray from showing around the edges. I'm getting a little old to lead Mercs. If I turned down a good offer, I might just not get another."

Just then a man came hurrying into the place. He was a tall, hardbitten man who wore the same kind of belted Merc coverall that they wore. He looked around and then hastened over to them.

"You're John Dilullo, aren't you?" he said. "I've seen you down at Merc Hall, though I never met you." He babbled, in his excitement. "We just found Bollard. Someone said you were in here, and I came—"

Dilullo had got to his feet and his face was suddenly twice as craggy and harsh. Bollard had been his second in the job they had last worked, and he was an old friend.

"You found him? What does that mean?"

"In an alley only a block or two from here," said the other. "Looks like he was stunned and robbed. We put in a call for the police and then someone said they'd seen you—"

Dilullo interrupted again, taking the babbling man by the arm and propelling him toward the door.

"Show me," he said.

He and Chane rapidly followed the man down the street. Darkness had fallen a little while ago, and the lights were on; the sidewalk was not yet too crowded.

The man kept babbling. "Don't think he's bad hurt, only stunned. I knew him right away, he was leader on a job I went on a year ago."

Dilullo muttered an oath. "I thought he was too old to be this sort of fool."

Their leader ducked into a narrow alley between looming warehouses. "This way . . . around the next corner. I don't know if the police are here yet. We called them first thing . . ."

They were halfway to the corner when from the darkness behind them came the whisper of a stunner, notched way down.

Dilullo dropped unconscious. Chane completed only a quarter of a turn before it dropped him too.

Chane was not unconscious. The stunner, to avoid being

too noisy, had been notched down to just the exact power sufficient to knock a man out.

An ordinary man, that is. But Chane was not an ordinary Earthman; Varna had bred tougher muscles and a tougher nervous system, and he did not go all the way out.

He fell and hit the pavement and lay there, face up, his eyes open, his limbs almost paralyzed. Almost. He could still move his muscles a bit, though they felt vague and remote.

He made no movement. The Starwolf cunning that a lifetime had fostered told him not to move yet, not until he had conquered at least some of the numbness.

As through a mist, he saw the man who had guided them here looking down at them, and then another man came running from whatever dark doorway he had hidden in for his ambush. Both men were wavering, unreal figures to Chane's eyes.

"This one," said the pseudo-Merc. He bent over Dilullo's unconscious figure and began to search him.

"I still don't think he'd have them on him," said the other man.

"Look," said the other, searching frantically. "He got six Kharali light-stones for his share of the last job and he hasn't been to any place to deposit them. I told you, I've been watching him . . . *ah!*"

He had drawn out from Dilullo's inner clothing a little pouch, and he shook its contents into his hand. Even in the darkness, the light-stones shone with that inner radiance that made the gem desired by all the galaxy.

Six jewels, Chane thought dully, and all Dilullo had gone through to get them, all that hell and danger in Corvus Cluster. The wise Dilullo, who kept his share in stones instead of selling them as Chane and the others had done.

Chane still made no movement. He could feel more life coming back into his nerves and muscles, but not enough yet. The other man bent over him and took his money

from his pocket, but he still did not move. He wasn't ready
. . .

Next moment he decided that he had to be ready. The
pseudo-Merc stood back and began to take off his coverall, and as he did so he spoke quickly to the other man.

"Cut their throats. They could both identify me. I'll
get this thing off and we'll get out of here."

The dark figure of the second man bent over Chane;
there was a gleam of steel in his hand.

Kill, Starwolf! thought Chane, and willed all his strength
into his half-numbed muscles.

He surged up and his hand moved and cracked across
the jaw of the man with the knife. He was half-numbed
and he didn't have all of his Varnan strength, but there was
enough to send the man with the knife reeling and falling.
And then the man was lying still.

Chane was already on his feet, staggering, unsure, but
going into his charge. The pseudo-Merc had his legs tangled
in the coverall he had been removing. He scrabbled in
his clothes for a hidden weapon, but Chane reached him
before he got it out.

The flat of Chane's hand struck across the pseudo-Merc's
throat. The man made a gulping sound, staggered, and fell
over. Chane fell too. He was too numb to stay erect, and
he lay for a few minutes before he could start to get up
again.

He had to rub his legs for minutes, with hands that felt
like mittens, before he could trust himself to stand. Then
he went over to one man and then the other, and looked at
them. They were hurt and unconscious, but they were not
dead.

Chane thought that if his strength hadn't been halved
by the stunner, they would have been killed. But maybe it
was just as well. Dilullo had this foolish prejudice against
unnecessary killing . . .

13

He went over to Dilullo and knelt and massaged the nerve-centers. Presently Dilullo came around.

The other Merc looked up dazedly. Chane said softly, "I thought that he was too old to be this sort of fool. Wasn't that what you said, John?"

Dilullo was taking it in by now. "You killed them?"

"I did not," Chane said. "I was a good little Merc. I have to admit it was because I wasn't strong enough, after taking the shock that knocked you cold."

"They were after my light-stones, of course," Dilullo said thickly. "I was a bloody fool to keep them on me, but I didn't think this could happen to me."

Chane retrieved the jewels and his own money.

"All right, let's move," said Dilullo. "We ought to drag them to the police, but law means delays and I don't think we want to hang around Earth courtrooms, with a job maybe coming up."

They went on through the alley and so into the bright streets again.

"John," said Chane.

"Yes?"

"I forgot to thank you for coming down to keep an eye on me."

Dilullo said nothing.

II

THE ENORMOUS CREAM-COLORED building that housed Ashton Trading was not too near the starport. It stood by itself in a wide space, in impressive aloofness. There was a big park for cars and fliers behind it, and a landscaped approach in front. Dilullo put coins in his auto-taxi and went inside, to an equally impressive interior of golden marble from a far starworld.

Officials, clerks, secretaries, bright of face and neatly dressed, came and went in quiet efficiency. They made Dilullo feel that his drab, belted coverall was distinctly out of place. But when a lift took him to the topmost level of offices, his reception was courtesy itself.

A rather exquisite young man offered a chair which Dilullo declined, and went into the inner offices. Looking around, Dilullo saw heads of girls and men looking at him from their desks. He heard the word "Merc".

Glamor, that's what I've got, thought Dilullo sourly. *I'm a Merc, an adventurer, somebody to look at.*

The hell of it was that he had once felt that way about it, when he was a very young man. He could have gone into interstellar trade and made money like the men who worked for the Ashtons, but that was too tame. He would be a Merc and people would look up to him.

And now here he was, middle-aged and worn around the edges, standing figuratively if not literally with hat in hand hoping for a good job from the traders he had once despised.

15

"Mr. Dilullo? This way, please."

He was ushered deferentially into a very big office whose wide windows looked out far across the starport quarter to the towers and docks and ships of the port itself.

Dilullo had his mental hackles up. He had had business with tycoons before and he did not like the type. He took James Ashton's proffered hand without enthusiasm.

"Thank you for coming, Mr. Dilullo," said Ashton. "I feel lucky that you are available."

Ashton, he conceded, did not look like a tycoon. He looked like a graying scholar of middle age, with a good face and friendly eyes and a certain awkwardness of manner.

Dilullo said bluntly, "Mr. Ashton, your secretary who contacted me said you had a job you'd like me to undertake. What job?"

And he thought, *Whatever it is, it's something real mean. Ashton Trading doesn't need Mercs for anything that isn't.*

Ashton took from a drawer a photograph which he handed over, a picture of a man some years younger than himself but with a strong resemblance.

"That's Randall Ashton, my brother. I want you to find him."

Dillullo looked up at him. "Find him? You mean you have no idea where he is?"

"I know where he is, in a general way," said Ashton. "He's in the Closed Worlds."

"The Closed Worlds?" Dilullo frowned. "I don't think I . . . wait a minute. Isn't there a star out beyond Perseus Arm with a triplet of planets . . . ?"

Ashton nodded. "The star Allubane. It has three planets —the Closed Worlds."

Dilullo's frown deepened. "Now I remember. A queer, isolated little system where they don't like visitors and kick out any who come. If you don't mind my asking, what the devil took your brother there?"

Ashton leaned back. "That takes a little explanation, Mr. Dilullo. But first let me say that while I know Randall is in the Closed Worlds, I don't know where he is in them, and I don't know whether he's alive or dead. It would be your job to find him and bring him back if he's living."

"Why do you need Mercs for that?" Dilullo asked skeptically. "Your firm has got hundreds of starships, thousands of good men working for you."

"Traders," said Ashton. "Not fighters. To get in and out of the Closed Worlds is going to be dangerous."

"But Government . . ."

"The Terran Government can't do a thing," Ashton answered. "It would be interfering with an independent starworld if it did. And the messages it sent to Allubane have just not been answered."

He spread out his hands. "You see now why I thought of the Mercs. They—and you in particular, Mr. Dilullo—have successfully performed some highly dangerous tasks. I've heard a great deal about you chaps."

"The Closed Worlds," muttered Dilullo. "I've heard something more about that system. It was a long time ago."

Yes, it was a long time ago. It was on my third Merc job, when I was young and proud as the devil of being a Merc. On Arcturus Two, and we'd just finished a job and made money. We felt good, and I sat there with the rest of them in the hot, steamy night, drinking the liquor that was far too strong for me, looking as casual as though I'd done this for a lifetime, listening to old Donahue talk.

Old Donahue? My God, I'm older now than Donahue was then, and where's it all gone—the youth and the careless money—and the friends? The little white night-bats they called iggin *kept darting in and out under the smoky lights, and I drank and looked as though it was all nothing to me— not the strange smells nor the sounds nor the slithery women who brought us drink, and all the time I was bursting with pride, I, the poor boy from Brindisi who had grabbed himself a handful of stars.*

What was it Donahue said about Allubane? "They've got something big there. Something so big they won't let anyone in lest it be taken away from them. They booted our behinds out of there as soon as we landed. Something damned big, there in the Closed Worlds."

"This business," Ashton was saying, "has been in our family for four generations. My father wanted to make sure it stayed that way. When Randall and I were youngsters, he sent us out—as ordinary crewmen, mind you—on a whole lot of star-trading voyages. It was supposed to teach us the business from the ground up."

Ashton shook his head. "With me, it worked. I learned, and I liked the business. I've been with it ever since. But with Randall, it turned out differently. He got fascinated by all the exotic, alien peoples he met on far starworlds. So fascinated that, despite my father's objections, he went back to university and took up extra-terrestrial anthropology. He's a first class expert in the field now."

"Is that what he's doing out at Allubane?" asked Dilullo.

Ashton nodded. "Randall had already made several field trips. Of course, having all the money he needs, he could afford to fit up his small outfits in the finest style. And on one of those trips he heard of some big scientific mystery in the Closed Worlds."

"Exactly what?"

"I don't know," Ashton said. "He wouldn't tell me, or anyone else. He said it was so fantastic that nobody would believe him until he brought back proof. For all I know, he may have been on a wild-goose chase.

"Anyway, he went. He got four specialists together, took a small cruiser and crew from the firm—you understand, he's a full partner—and out he went to Allubane. He hasn't come back."

18

Ashton paused. "Well, that's it. Not a word from him for five months. I don't know what he's doing there, but I want to know, and I'm willing to pay a Merc party to go out and find him. There may be big trouble or no trouble at all. Just find him."

"What if we find him dead?" asked Dilullo.

"In that case, I'll want you to bring back legal proof of his death."

"I see."

Ashton said, "You don't see. Get that look off your face. I love my brother and I want him safe. But if he *is* dead, I've got to know it—I can't run a big business when nobody knows whether the co-owner of the business is alive or dead."

Dilullo said soberly, "Mr. Ashton, I would like to apologize for what I just implied."

Ashton nodded. "It's understandable. Business men, if they're successful, are supposed to be a combination of wolf and shark. But Randall's a fine man, and I'm worried about him."

He reached into his desk and brought out a folder which he handed to Dilullo. "I've had prepared all that's known about Allubane's worlds. Our company's pretty well briefed on most starworlds, but even so, it's scanty. I assume you'd like to study this before making a decision about taking the job."

Dilullo nodded, and took the folder. He started to rise, saying, "I'll take this and read it."

"Read it now," said Ashton. "That is, you have the time. Nothing is more important to me right now than Randall."

Dilullo was surprised. He picked up the folder and began to read the pages in it, while Ashton worked quietly with his papers.

Dilullo's long face got longer, as he read. *This is a sour one*, he thought. *It's no good, no good at all. Turn it down.*

And have them say that John Dilullo's getting too old for the tough jobs?

He read the material through, then went back and read some parts of it again, and then slowly closed the folder.

Ashton looked up, and Dilullo said slowly, "Mr. Ashton, this would be a nasty job. I hope you'll believe that I'm not saying that so I can run the price up on you."

Ashton nodded. "I believe you. I couldn't hold this chair if I couldn't size up men. Go ahead."

"I'll give you my honest opinion," said Dilullo. "I think your brother's dead."

He tapped the folder. "Look at what you have here. There's the fact that these people of Arkuu, the main one of the three planets of Allubane, won't have strangers on their worlds. Anybody lands there, they run them right out. It's been that way since starships first landed there.

"All right," Dilullo continued. "Your brother went there months ago. If the Arkuuns had run him out, you'd have heard from him long ago. But you didn't. Yet this record shows they've never let a living stranger stay there. The obvious conclusion is that he's dead."

Ashton had a sadness in his face as he said, "I'm afraid you have logic on your side. But I can't just accept logic, with my brother out there, perhaps needing help badly. I've got to find out."

He went on. "I read all that material. I realize the danger involved. All I can do is say that I'll pay well for the risk. All your expenses, and five hundred thousand Earth dollars fee if you bring back Randall or definite information as to his fate."

And, Dilullo thought, *a Merc leader's share is one-fifth, and the ship-owner's share a fifth, and the rest share alike. That's a hundred thousand and that's the big, beautiful house above Brindisi that I've wanted all my life.*

He said "That's an awful lot of money."

"It's Ashton Trading money," said Ashton. "Which means

it's Randall's as much as mine. Maybe it can help him. What about it, Dilullo?"

Dilullo thought, but not for very long. He could see the house, the white walls and the portico, the flaming flowers spilling down the slope in front of it.

"I'll take on the job," he said. "But I'm not the only one, remember. I have to get a bunch of Mercs to go with me, and I've got to show them this material. I never led men into danger without warning them. I don't know if I can convince them, even for that money."

Ashton stood up. "Fair enough. I'll have the contracts drawn up, in the hopes that you can."

Dilullo hesitated a split second, not knowing whether or not he should offer to shake hands with as important a man as this one, but Ashton simply stuck out his hand.

All the way back to the hotel Dilullo kept thinking about a hundred thousand dollars. He clung to the thought because he had a growing feeling in his bones that he had taken on a job that was just too big and tough for Mercs.

Chane was waiting in the hotel room.

"What about the job?" he asked.

"It's a sweet one," said Dilullo. "It's big, and the money's real big. All I have to do is convince a dozen Mercs to lose all their good sense and go with me."

He told Chane. Chane stiffened, and an odd look came into his dark face.

"Allubane?"

"Yes. It's a star in the Perseus Arm and it has three planets."

"I know where it is," said Chane. He began to laugh a little. "So much for Varna law. I'm going to Allubane."

Dilullo stared. "What's this? Do you know anything about the Closed Worlds?"

"Not much," said Chane. "But years ago they heard on Varna that there was something big, something terrific,

21

guarded by the people of that planet Arkuu, so a raiding Varnan squadron went there."

"What did they find?"

Chane shook his head. "They didn't say, not to anybody except the Council. They came back with nothing at all. But then the Council decreed that no Varnans were ever to go back to Allubane—that it was too dangerous a place."

Dilullo simply stared at him in silence until the impact of Chane's words really hit him.

If the Starwolves, who feared neither man nor God nor devil, were afraid of something at Allubane, that something had to be big and dangerous.

"Ah, you would come up with something like this," he said. "If this gets around, I'll never be able to sign a Merc for this mission. Do me a favor, will you, Chane? Go away somewhere, for a little while."

"Where?"

"You said once you'd like to see where your parents come from on Earth. It's a place in Wales, you said. You can get there quick."

Chane considered. "I think I will. I don't much like this place."

"And Chane," said Dilullo. "Don't come back till I call you. You almost Jonahed the last job; I'm damned if I'll have you Jonah this one."

III

CHANE WALKED THE STREETS of the old town, narrow ways, with low buildings, that slanted down toward the sea. The day was dark with great clouds and a mist and spume blew in from the ocean; the worn stones under his feet were wet and glistening. The wind was raw and boisterous, muttering of coming gales.

He liked this place. It was almost as grim and harsh as Varna. And he liked the people, though they had looked at him with neither any particular friendship nor hostility. He suddenly realized that it was their voices he liked. They talked in a queer, lilting way, just the way his father had talked, and he remembered that his father had called it the "singsong."

There did not seem to be very much in this small place of Carnarvon, except a big hulking wreck of a castle down by the sea, so he went that way. The place was ancient and battered but had a sort of grandeur under the stormy sky. There was an old man in a uniform coat at the gate who sold tickets. Chane bought a ticket and started in.

Then he thought of something, and went back and asked, "I wonder if you could tell me something. You've lived here a long time, I take it?"

"All my life," said the old man. He had short, snow-white hair and a bony red face, and surprisingly bright blue eyes which he fixed on Chane.

"Some of my family came from here," Chane said. "I

wondered if you knew anything about them. A Reverend Thomas Chane, who grew up here in Carnarvon."

"Caernarfon, we Welsh call it," said the old man. "It means 'fortress in Arfon.' And well I remember the Reverend Thomas. He was a fine young man, devoted to the Lord, and he went away to the stars to convert some wicked heathen and died there. Are you his son?"

Caution stirred in Chane. It was the fact that he had been born on Varna that had made him a Starwolf, and he didn't want talk about that going around.

"Just a nephew," he said.

"Ah, then you'll be David Chane's son, that went away to America," nodded the old man. "I am William Williams, and I am glad indeed to meet one from the old families who had come back."

He ceremoniously shook hands with Chane. "Yes, yes, the Reverend Thomas was a fine man and a strong preacher. I do not doubt that he converted many out on that distant world before the Lord took him."

Chane only nodded, but as he passed on into the castle he was remembering his father on Varna. The little chapel where there was never any congregation except some Varnan children who came in to listen to the Earthman who spoke their language so poorly. His father's small figure valiantly erect and his face aglow as he preached, and his mother playing the small electronic organ, both of them dying slowly as Varna's heavy gravitation slowly dragged the life out of them, but neither of them admitting it, neither of them willing to quit and go back to Earth.

He walked around and found that the looming castle was really only a hollow shell, a great open space inside it. He climbed the towers and the battlements of the walls, and wondered what it would have been like to fight in the way that they did, back in the far past, with swords and spears and primitive weapons. He supposed that some of his own ancestors had been fighters like that.

He mused, liking the lowering sky and the harsh old stones and the silence, until William Williams came to him, wearing now a worn wool jacket instead of the uniform coat.

"We close now," said the old man. "I'll walk up through town with you and show you a few of our sights . . . it's on my way."

As they walked, with the sky dusking into twilight, it seemed that the old chap was more interested in asking questions than in answering them.

"And you came from America? Of course, that was where David went, long ago. Is it a good job you have there?"

"I'm not there very much," Chane said. "I've worked in starships for a long time."

He thought how Dilullo would react to that discreet description of a Starwolf's profession, and smiled a little.

"Ah, it's a wonderful thing that men can go to the stars but it's not for me, not for me," said William Williams. He stopped, and steered Chane toward the door of a low stone building. "We'll have a pint together, if you'll so honor me."

The room inside was low and poorly lit, and there was no one but a barman and three young men farther along the bar.

Williams paid for the pint with the utmost dignity, insisting, "It is my pleasure, to buy an ale for one of the Chanes."

Chane thought the stuff was mild as water but he did not want to say so. He suggested having another, and the old man dug an elbow into his ribs in a roguish sort of way, saying, "Well, since you've twisted my arm, I must break my usual rule."

When that was finished he took Chane along the bar to the three young men and told them, "This is the son of David Chane of Caernarfon, and you've all heard of that family. And these are Hayden Jones and Griff Lewis and Lewis Evans."

25

They mumbled acknowledgment to Chane. Two of them were small and nondescript young men but Hayden Jones was a very big, dark young man with very bright, black eyes.

"And now I must say good night and be getting along," the old man told Chane. "I leave you in good company and hope you come home again."

Chane said goodbye, then turned to the three young men and suggested that he buy them a drink.

There was a furtive hostility about them, and they did not answer him. He repeated the offer.

"We do not need damned Americans coming here to buy our ale for us," said Hayden Jones without looking at him.

"Ah," said Chane. "That may be true. But you need better manners, don't you?"

The big young man whirled and his hand cracked and Chane found himself, amazed, sitting on the floor of the room. The old Starwolf anger flared up in him bright as fire, and he gathered himself.

Then he saw Hayden Jones turn to his two companions, not saying anything but on his face the pleased smile of a child who had just made everyone notice him. There was something so naive in that smile that the bright anger faded away as fast as it had come.

Chane relaxed his muscles and got to his feet. He rubbed his chin and said, "You have a hard hand on you, Hayden Jones."

He stuck out his hand and grasped Jones' shoulder in a bruising grip, putting his Varna strength into it. "I have a hard hand too. If it's a fight you must have I'll oblige you. But what I would really like to do is buy a few drinks."

Hayden Jones looked startled, and then he grinned sheepishly and looked at his two companions. "Well, now," he said. "We can always fight later, can't we, after we've had those drinks?"

They had the drinks, and then they had some more, and

when the barman finally shoved them out the door it was late night and the gale had broken. The wind threw rain at them like smallshot as they went down the slanting streets, singing the songs that Chane's three companions had been trying to teach him.

An upstairs window opened and an elderly female's voice screeched at them. Hayden Jones turned and shouted, with great stateliness.

"Be quiet, is it? And when, Mrs. Griffith, have you been so unpatriotic that you cannot hear the national anthem of Wales?"

The window slammed down and they went on. Outside the hotel, Hayden Jones said, "Now, about the fight . . ."

"Let us save it until next time," said Chane. "Late at night, I have no stomach for it."

"Until next time!"

They grinned at each other and shook hands. Chane went inside and up to his room. When he got there the little communic he had placed on the old-fashioned wooden bureau was buzzing. He switched it on, and John Dilullo's voice came through.

"Chane? You can come back now. I've got a crew."

Chane acknowledged, feeling a strong sense of regret. Ancestral memories or not, he had taken a liking to this place and these people. He would have wished to stay longer. But he was obedient, and booked his passage on the first New York rocket. All the way across the Atlantic he was thinking, *I will come back to that place some day and have that fight. I think it would be a good one.*

Back in New York, Chane went into the building on a side street in the starport quarter that was formally the Headquarters of the Guild of Mercenaries, but which was always called Merc Hall.

In the big main room he looked up at the wall where the crews were posted. There were neat directories of white letters on black backgrounds. He read the first one.

Leader: Martin Bender
Second: J. Bioc
Ship-captain: Paul Vristow

There followed under that a dozen other names, some of which were not Earthman names at all. Then, below that;

Destination: Procyon Three.

He went along the wall, reading the other directories, and he thought, Achernar, Vanoon, Spica, Morr, the Mercs really got around. Until he saw

Leader: John Dilullo
Second: J. Bollard

And on with the other names. "Morgan Chane" was at the bottom of the list.

Dilullo's voice rasped in his ear. "Well, did you expect to be first? Remember, you're a pretty new Merc. You have no seniority."

"I'm surprised," said Chane, "that Bollard would go out again this soon."

Dilullo smiled bleakly. "Bollard's one of the few Mercs who's a family man. He's got a raft of children he adores. He's also got an ugly, nagging wife. He stays home just long enough to turn over his takings and then gets out to space again."

Dilullo added, "We're made up. I'm going to call Mr. Ashton; if he's free, I'll go over and sign the contract. Wait here."

Chane waited, and presently Dilullo came back with a surprised look on his face.

"You know what? Ashton's coming over here. He said he wants to meet the whole crew."

Dilullo, impressed, hurried out to get the crew together in one of the smaller rooms of the Hall. Bollard came in and saw Chane, and his fat, round face creased in an affectionate smile.

"Ah, the rock-hopper," he said. "I saw your name on the list, Chane. I haven't decided yet whether I'm happy about it."

"Be happy," said Chane.

Bollard shook his head, laughing as though he'd heard the best joke in the world. "No, I'm not sure. You nearly jammed us into big trouble the last time, though I have to admit you did noble helping to get us out of it."

"Mr. James Ashton," said Dilullo's voice, speaking gruffly as though he refused to be impressed by a very important person.

Ashton smiled and nodded and went through the introductions. The Mercs were all as polite as Sunday-school scholars. They eyed the man of money with unliking eyes.

Then Ashton surprised them. He began to talk to them, looking a little bit upset and embarrassed, but very earnest and determined, like a fussy schoolteacher trying to explain something.

"I've been worrying about you men," he said. "I offered a big lot of money for men to go to the Closed Worlds and look for my brother, and I know the money is why you're going. But I feel worried . . ."

He broke off, and then resolutely started again. "I've been thinking: I may be endangering a lot of men's lives, to save the one life of my brother. So I thought I should tell you . . . this job will be dangerous, as I'm sure Mr. Dilullo has explained. But if it's too dangerous, I want no man's death on my conscience. If the risks are too great, draw back. If you come back and tell me that it was not within reason to go on, I'll still pay two thirds of what I offered."

The Mercs said nothing but there was a sudden thaw in their attitude. Finally Dilullo said, "Thanks, Mr. Ashton. Mercs don't quit very easily. But thanks, just the same."

When Ashton and the other Mercs had gone, Dilullo told Chane, "You know, Ashton's a good sort. The fact that he made an offer like that, that he's worried about us, will make us knock ourselves out for him at Allubane."

Chane said, with an ironical smile, "Sure it will. And maybe that's just why he said that."

Dilullo looked at him disgustedly. "I wouldn't have a Starwolf's mind for anything you can name. No wonder that you don't really have a friend in the universe."

"But I have," said Chane. "I made some, in the place called Wales. Fine fellows, full of fight and fun, and they taught me some great songs. Listen to this one—it's an old war-song about the Men of Harlech."

He threw back his head and sang, and Dilullo winced.

"There's never been anybody Welsh who didn't fancy he could sing," he said. "Not even a Starwolf."

"It's a grand tune," said Chane. "It's worthy of being a Varnan battle-song."

"Then get ready to sing it in the Closed Worlds," Dilullo said. "I've got a feeling that my greed for money and a fine house is taking us to big trouble there."

IV

THE LITTLE MERC SHIP, a Class Twenty, plodded out through the system of Sol and then jumped into overdrive and went on its way.

The vast, sweeping spirals of the galaxy, the irregularly curved arms of denser star-concentrations, dwarfed the ship to a mere infinitesimal mote. Far behind it, Cygnus Arm was a gigantic rampart of gleaming suns. It stretched in a rimward direction to a galactic latitude of twenty degrees, then split off into two almost equally awesome continents of stars, the Vela Spur and Orion Spur.

The ship moved on and on, putting the great mass of Orion Spur behind it, swinging past an elongated tangle of "hot hydrogen" clouds, heading toward the glittering sprawl of Perseus Arm, nearly at the rim. It did not move in a completely straight course, even in overdrive. The wheel of stars that was the galaxy was a rotating wheel, and relative positions altered constantly, and then the computers would clack and talk among themselves and change the course a little.

In the bridge, Kimmel, the captain and co-owner of the craft, looked at the rep-chart's gleaming lights.

"Everything seems all right," he said to Dilullo.

The slight emphasis on "seems" was characteristic. Kimmel was a small, bald, nervous man who worried about things nearly all the time. He worried mostly about the ship taking any damage.

Lots of Merc leaders had got so bored with Kimmel's worrying that they wouldn't sign with him. But Dilullo had known him a long while, and preferred a worrying captain to a carefree one. He knew that Kimmel, if anything threatened his precious ship, would fight like a lion.

"Sure it's all right," he said. "Nothing to it. Just take us out to Perseus Arm and break out within normal-drive distance of Allubane."

"And what then?" said Kimmel. "Have you looked at the S-Chart of that Allubane system? Rotten with drift, and the radar will likely be all fouled up by radio emissions from the hydrogen clouds there."

"Cool hydrogen," Dilullo interrupted.

"I know, I know; it's supposed to emit only on the twenty-first centimeter band, but if there's gas debris colliding with it, cool hydrogen can blow the radar faster than hot. And suppose it does just that?"

"Suppose nothing of the sort," said Dilullo soothingly. "Just remember, Kimmel, I'm not going to do anything reckless—my skin is as dear to me as this old tub is to you."

"Old tub?" cried Kimmel. He began an angry statement. Dilullo went away, a slight smile on his hard face. He had been steering Kimmel away from his worries by that approach for a long time, and the captain had not caught on yet.

In his small cabin, Dilullo got out the papers that James Ashton had given him and studied them.

He thought about four people.

Dr. Martin Garcia, of the Cuernavaca School of Extra-Terrestrial Anthropology; S. Sattargh, exchange instructor from the University of Arcturus Three; Jewett McGoun, formerly a free-lance interstellar trader; and Dr. Jonas Caird of the Foundation of Extra-Terrestrial Sciences in New York.

He looked the names over again. There was one of them that did not seem to fit.

Jewett McGoun, free star-trader. What was he doing with four scientists?

Dilullo read further in the notes that James Ashton had made for him. And after a while he muttered, "Ah-huh."

It was Jewett McGoun who had first told Randall Ashton about something big and wonderful in the Closed Worlds. He had, so Randall had averred, brought solid evidence of his story. But Randall would not show this evidence to his brother and he would not tell the exact nature of what he was going after.

"You wouldn't believe me," Randall Ashton had said. "But I'll tell you how big it is—it could absolutely revolutionize the exploration of the universe."

More than that he would not say. And so they had gone eagerly off to Allubane . . . four questing scientists and Mr. Jewett McGoun.

It smelled, Dilullo thought. It smelled at him right off the pages of these notes.

There had long been a story, told by many another like old Donahue, of a great secret in the Closed Worlds. It probably had been dreamed up just because the Closed Worlds *were* closed.

But take that story and build on it, contrive phony evidence, then present the whole thing to an enthusiastic student of the extra-terrestrial who also happened to be a millionaire, and you could toll him off to Allubane. And once you had him there, there were a good many different ways by which you might enrich yourself from him.

But if McGoun had only been selling a phony story about something big in the Closed Worlds, why did the Starwolves fear to go there?

"Ah, curse that Chane," muttered Dilullo. "He can spoil anything, even a good theory."

The ship went on and on, for one ship-day after another, and it seemed that it was going to rush through overdrive for an eternity, until finally there came a time when the siren hooted.

Dilullo thought, *It's about time,* and went up from his cabin, heading for the bridge. He passed the small cubby where Chane was doing substitute duty for the radar man.

He stuck his head in and said, "You haven't been bored, have you, Chane?"

Chane gave him a bright smile. "Now why would I be bored? Here I am, in a ship going almost half as fast as a Varnan ship would go, crawling along, at a pretty good clip. Why in the world would I be bored?"

Dilullo grinned a little. "That's good to hear. But just in case you *have* been bored, I rather imagine there'll be some action soon. And, Chane . . ."

"Yes?"

"You'll be happy to know that if there is any action, anything really dangerous, I'll see to it that you're right in the forefront. Are you grateful?"

Chane said between his teeth, "I'm grateful, you old so-and-so."

Dilullo was laughing a little when he reached the bridge. He had no sooner reached it than the siren hooted the second warning. He grabbed a stanchion as the ship went out of overdrive.

The lights went dim and the whole fabric of the vessel seemed to shudder and dissolve. So did Dilullo's personal being. No matter how often he went through this, he never lost the moment of panic fear, the conviction that his shredded atoms were dispersed for all time and could never be gathered again. It was like the old ancestral falling-dream, only infinitely worse. Then, as always, they hit bottom, the transition was over, and they were in normal space again.

They were just outside the edge of the Perseus Arm. It was one thing to call it that, to mark it on the map as one of the outer spirals of the galaxy. It was another thing to be there, to look out the viewport at the titanic coast of stars, high as heaven and flaring as hell.

"Now, David," said Kimmel. "Now let us go on."

Dave Mattock, the pilot, shoved the control levers and the ship started moving toward the nearest star in the Arm, a topaz-colored sun.

Mattock was renowned among Mercs for two reasons. One was that he chewed tobacco. Hardly anyone had used tobacco in any form for a long time; there were mild drugs that were much safer and just as sedative. Almost no one had actually chewed the stuff for decades, but as a boy, Mattock had been taught the habit by a rapscallion old grandfather in the Kentucky hills, and he had never given it up.

The other reason Mattock was famous was that he had never lost his temper with Kimmel. It had been said often in Merc Hall that when Mattock quit piloting, Kimmel would have to retire, for no other pilot would be able to take the worrying captain.

"Easy, easy!" cried Kimmel. "We've got to take this system carefully. Remember what I told you about those cool hydrogen clouds. And that drift . . . that terrific drift . . ."

Mattock, a large powerful man with a large, rock-jawed face, paid not the slightest attention. He chewed, and he moved the controls.

"Godalmighty, David, are you trying to pile us up?" cried Kimmel. He was almost dancing up and down now, leaning over Mattock's shoulder, reading the dials, not quite wringing his hands but almost doing that. "We've lots of time, lots of time . . ."

Mattock spat, with ringing accuracy, at the plastic pail in the corner that was a fixture when he was on the bridge. He said nothing.

"Ah, that's it . . . that's it . . . careful does it," squeaked Kimmel. "After all, David, we want to be careful, don't we? That's a good careful boy . . ."

Mattock read the computer figures flaring across the screen and calmly punched down on the power.

There came from Kimmel a squeal like that of a stricken rabbit; he clutched his hands over his bald head like an old woman awaiting doomsday.

Dilullo grinned. He had had a good many landings with Kimmel and Mattock and they had never changed much.

He looked out ahead. They were running down fast toward Allubane, and the topaz sun glared bright and wicked in his eyes.

The computer began to stutter now and then. The emissions from the cool hydrogen clouds one couldn't even see were interfering with radar information, and without information the computers were just metal and wire and crystals. Useless.

Dust whispered along the hull. They were getting into the edges of the drift and it was bad—not the worst, but bad enough. It always made Dilullo wish that the suns and planets were as clean and tidy as they looked on the star-charts, with nothing between them but nice, clean open space. But it wasn't that way at all; their making had left many of them a bit messy around the edges. In time the debris would be all swept up by their gravitational fields, but human beings didn't have that kind of time.

The whispering became a crackling, outside the hull. Kimmel went and buried his face against the wall of the bridge-room. Dilullo watched him admiringly. This was the next-to-last phase for him, the "I can't look" phase.

The crackling outside the hull eased, then came back again, a little stronger. The computers went off for a whole minute, a silence that was dread-inspiring.

Kimmel came away from the wall. He came and sat down in the co-pilot chair. He sat quite still, his head stuck forward, his eyes stony, a little glazed, his shoulders hunched.

Dilullo nodded to himself. This was the final phase, the "All is lost, sunk in despair" phase.

Mattock calmly turned his head and spat regally into the bucket.

The computers came back on again and the crackle of drift faded; before them there came into view three planets, two on this side of the star and the third halfway around it.

Dilullo thought, it was like that which Berlioz had written about the second movement of Beethoven's Fourth Symphony: ". . . the great chords come up like newly-created worlds swimming up, fresh and beautiful from the hand of God."

He felt proud of himself for a moment; no other Merc captain would know things like that. And then he thought forlornly, *But I only know them because I was alone and lonely for so long, and so much time to read.*

He looked at the Closed Worlds as one looks at the eyes of an enemy. And they went on down toward the smoky yellow flare of Allubane.

V

CHANE SMELLED DANGER in the silence.

He stood with a half-dozen other Mercs on the battered spaceport in front of their ship. The hot lemon-colored sunlight poured down and the warm wind whispered around them; there was no other sound.

The massive white marble city beyond the spaceport climbed a slope in tier after tier of ancient-looking buildings. It was too far away to be heard, and the silence did not bother Chane. But here on the spaceport it was too quiet. There was no movement at the warehouses and other buildings. The eight or nine small planetary cruisers near them, four of which had missile-launcher ports in their sides, had no activity around them.

"Just take it easy," said Dilullo. "Be casual. It's safer to wait and let them make the first move."

Milner, beside Chane, muttered, "It would be safer still by a damn sight to be wearing our stunners."

Milner was a foul-mouthed, fighty little man whom none of the other Mercs liked much, and who got berths only because of his superlative skill in using and servicing weapons. Yet Chane had to agree with him.

But Dilullo had been dogmatic about it. They had to come in to Allubane One—its planet-name was Arkuu—and take its people by surprise, but they mustn't seem to be looking for a fight.

They had managed the surprise all right. They had homed

in on the other side of Arkuu, and then had whipped half around the planet toward this capital city of Yarr without sending any notice of arrival or requesting landing-permission.

Chane had looked down on Arkuu as it rolled rapidly away beneath them, and thought it was not much of a world.

Crimson jungle covered a lot of it. Here and there, where the land rose into dark mountains, the jungle gave way to forests of deeper red. Once there was an ocher-colored sea, with tawny rivers snaking into it.

And cities. Cities of white marble that had been great and gracious once, but now were whelmed by the red tide of the jungle. Cities with no life stirring in their broken stones, the wrecks of the past, brooding under the topaz sun like old, dead kings whose glory is long forgotten.

Chane felt a sharply heightened sense of the mystery of this far world. Once its people must have been great indeed, to build such cities and to have gone out and colonized the second planet. What was it that had made them throw it all away? What was it that made them set their faces against interstellar travel, so that they made their system into the Closed Worlds?

Then their ship had come over the ridge of a valley and below them was another white city but this one still living, with people and a few ground-cars moving in its streets and some light fixed-wing fliers buzzing in the sky. With no warning at all, they had landed at the little planetary spaceport.

And now they waited, with Bollard and Kimmel and four others inside the ship just in case, and the sun was hot and nothing was happening.

Dilullo spoke without turning. "I'll do the talking."

A ground-car had emerged from the city and was coming across the spaceport toward them. It stopped a little way from them and two men got out of it and approached.

Chane, looking at the men, felt a sharp surprise.

He had expected the people of this decayed civilization to be limp, effete, weak. But these two were as impressive as he had ever seen.

They were tall, wide-shouldered, powerful-looking men, with pale golden skins and deep yellow hair and eyes of an icy blue-green. They wore short belted jerkins that left arms and legs bare, exposing superb muscles. They were about the least effete-looking men Chane had ever encountered.

One of the two, the younger and taller one, spoke to Dilullo in galacto, the lingua-franca of the galaxy. He spoke it a bit rustily.

"You are not welcome here," he said flatly. "Did you not know that the Closed Worlds are . . . closed?"

Dillullo gave him a straight answer. "We knew it."

"Then why did you come here?"

"I would like to give my reasons to those in your government with authority."

The younger man said, "We come from government and speak for it. I am Helmer and this is Bros. Now speak—why did you land here?"

Dilullo squared his shoulders as though he knew that he was heading into it now, but there was no way out of it.

"We came to look for a man," he said. "An Earthman, Randall Ashton by name, and his companions."

The two Arkuuns were silent for a moment. Chane saw them glance at each other, and then the one named Helmer answered.

"The man you look for is not here."

"Then where is he?"

Helmer shrugged. "Who knows? He was here, and then he went away."

"To one of the other two planets?"

Helmer merely shrugged his broad shoulders again. "Who knows?"

Chane thought, *I'd like to try knocking the answer out of him. The muscles he's got he'd give even a Varnan a tussle.*

As though he caught the thought, or detected it from Chane's expression, the tall young Arkuun suddenly looked directly at him. It was as though, towering and great-limbed as he was, he recognized a potential powerful antagonist in the compact figure and dark, faintly mocking face of Chane.

Then he turned back to Dilullo. "You are to go," he said. "We cannot service starships here, but we can give you food and water. Take them and go."

"Now wait a minute," said Dilullo. "You may be hermits here, but there are certain rules in the civilized starworlds about the right of repatriation of nationals. If you knew more about the galaxy as it is, you'd realize . . ."

He was interrupted by Bros, the older man, who laughed suddenly. His laughter was loud and nervous, oddly mirthless.

"Did you hear that, Helmer?" he said. "If we Arkuuns only knew more about the universe. But he is right. Our people have never been anywhere, have they?"

He laughed again, and a sardonic smile came onto Helmer's strong face.

To Chane, there was something ominous, hidden, in this sudden mirth. But it stung Dilullo.

"Let me tell you something," he said in an edged voice. "This man Randall Ashton is an important man, and comes from people with power. If I go back and report that you won't even tell what's happened to him, you'll sooner or later have a force come here that'll knock the Closed Worlds wide open."

Helmer's face became instantly stone cold. "Ah," he said. "Is it so?"

Chane groaned inwardly and thought, *Your foot slipped that time, John—a Starwolf child would have known better.*

41

He felt like shaking Dilullo. He looked away, toward the city, and his eye was caught by a point of light that came and went in one of the taller buildings, where a window that seemed to be swinging in the wind caught and reflected the lemon sunlight.

"Since you make threats," Helmer was saying icily, "I too will threaten. Go now, or you do not go at all."

He turned his back on Dilullo, and he and Bros went to their car and sped away.

Dilullo turned around and looked sourly at the Mercs. "Right up against a blank wall," he said. "Well, your peerless leader isn't doing so good. Anybody got any ideas?"

"I've got one," Chane said. "I'd get back in the ship and go out of here as though the devil was riding our tail."

Dilullo stared at him, as though a Chane counseling flight was a new and upsetting phenomenon.

Chane explained, with insulting carefulness. "You told him that if you got back and made your report, it would bring big trouble on them. *If* you got back."

It sank in. The Mercs looked from Chane to Dilullo, and Dilullo's face became longer.

"You're right," he said. "I tried a bluff and it didn't work, and we've bought it if we stay here. Emergency take-off."

They ran into the ship. The locks slammed shut, and within a minute the hooter blared its warning. Mattock took them skyward with a slamming rush. The friction-alarms started screeching like hysterical women, but Mattock ignored them. Presently they were out of atmosphere.

Chane had gone to his post at radar; he scanned the planet falling away behind them. Presently he saw what he expected to see.

"Two Arkuun ships coming out fast after us," he said, and added, "I think we can expect some missiles."

"Up shields," Dilullo ordered, and then swore. "We may have made it easier for them. They wouldn't have dared use those missiles on the spaceport, so close to the city."

"Shields up," came Bollard's voice.

The ship rocked to a *blam-blam* impact, and Bollard added, "And about time."

It did not look too good to Chane. The Merc ship had no launchers; its shields were light ones and would not take a prolonged hammering.

Kimmel was hanging over Mattock's chair and now he began talking to him. Chane expected more worried wailing, but he did not know Kimmel the way Dilullo did, and was surprised.

"Now, David," Kimmel was saying, "we have to shake those cruisers off fast. If a screen fails, we can take damage. Costly damage." He quivered a little like a nervous terrier as he said that. "So you head for that stream of drift zenithward from Allubane Two."

Mattock looked up at him. "Hit the drift?"

"Yes, David, it's our best chance. I saw those ships at the spaceport; they're old types and can't have radar as good as ours. We can throw them off in the drift; they won't chance it for long. But with our good radar you can take us on through, David."

Mattock spat mightily and said, "Hit the drift. Okay."

The ship veered sharply. Chane watched the radar screen. They were hauling away from the Arkuun cruisers, but not fast enough to get clear out of missile range. He told that to Dilullo.

"Ah, I played the devil with my smart bluff," Dilullo muttered. "And we didn't even find out if Ashton's party are alive or dead."

"Some of them are alive," Chane said.

"How do you know?"

Chane did not turn from the screen as he said, "A window up in one of those bigger buildings in the city kept swinging and reflecting sunlight. It was blinking 'ASHTON' in ship code."

"You didn't tell me that," Dilullo accused.

Chane smiled. "I didn't want to tell you anything that might distract you from pulling tail fast."

A salvo hit the screens and the ship rocked wildly. The thunderous noise drowned Dilullo's answer to that.

Chane was just as glad.

VI

THEY WERE IN THE drift now, and it was bad. It was so bad that Kimmel kept his mouth completely shut, which was always a sign of danger. The computers clacked and worried as they ran on down toward Allubane Two.

They passed zenithward of that spinning planet. It looked to Chane not unlike Arkuu, except that the jungles were forest on this second planet, and rather thin forest at that. There were none of the ancient white marble cities, but more modest towns of stone. Lights shone here and there from the dark side of the planet.

Chane scanned the screen. "They've broken off pursuit."

Kimmel looked at Dilullo. "Now what? Do we head back to Sol? Remember, John, we get two-thirds of the money just for trying. We certainly tried."

Dilullo looked at him bleakly. "We didn't do anything. I tried a stupid bluff and we had to hightail it out of there. You think I want to take a story like that back to Merc Hall?"

"But what, then . . . . ?"

"We're going back to Arkuu," Dilullo said decisively. "But in a different way. Head out of this system, get Allubane Three between us and the primary, and then swing back and land on that planet."

"Allubane Three? But it's supposed to be uninhabited, nothing much there at all."

"Exactly the kind of place we need, so set down there," said Dilullo.

The ship went on, edging out of the drift. It went beyond the third planet, which was a tawny, barren-looking ball, and then swung back again, running up the planet-shadow.

They came down upon a world that was almost desert, a world with bitter-looking seas and sad, barren lands with scant vegetation and no sign of people at all. Mattock brought them down near a seashore and cut the power.

"Very well done, David," said Kimmel.

"Get the launchers out and set them up," said Dilullo on the intercom, and rattled off names.

Chane's was one of them and he went down into the hold. They squeezed and tugged, hauling the portable missile-launchers past the stored skitter-flier and ground-car, manhandling them out of the cargo port.

The air was cold. This was the outermost of the Closed Worlds, and the sun had little warmth in it. They set up the launchers, and then stood by them, keeping an eye on the sky.

Chane and the Merc named Van Fossan manned one of the launchers. Van Fossan was a lean, blond, thirtyish young Hollander, with an eager eye and a face like a young hound's.

"What do you think John will do now?" he asked Chane.

Chane shrugged. What he wanted to say was that Dilullo should get his brains back into his head from where he had been carrying them, but an odd feeling of loyalty forbade him voicing the thought.

"No people, but some life here," said Van Fossan a little later. "Look at that."

The smoky yellow flare of Allubane was setting out over the ocean. Van Fossan pointed to two black, big, snaky-looking winged things flying out there. He added,

"... *when sunset, like a crimson throat to Hell,*
Is cavernous, she marks the seaward flight

Of homing dragons dark upon the west."

Chane looked at him. "What do you mean? That sky isn't crimson; it's dark yellow."

"It's a poem," Van Fossan said, and added disgustedly, "English is your mother tongue. Don't you know your own poetry?"

"I don't know many poems," said Chane. "I know some songs . . ." He broke off, and his lips twitched.

No, he thought. *I will not sing those songs for Nico. They were the songs we sang on Varna when the raiding squadrons were in, and they would not be good for Earthman ears.*

He dreamed again of Varna. Would he ever go there again? He felt somehow that he would, though it might be going to his death. The brothers of Ssander, whom he had killed in the fair fight that had got him chased out of the Starwolves, would never forgive him.

The yellow sky darkened to a dusky saffron, but no ships appeared in it.

"Chane," said Van Fossan in a low voice. "Look."

Chane turned his attention from the sky to the barren landscape around them.

Then he saw. A furry, dark animal about the size and look of a bear but with six limbs, was industriously digging out a bush only a few hundred feet from them. There were three more of the animals, but they were much farther away.

The creature dug out the bush and started chewing on its root. It looked with mild, stupid eyes as it did so, and then it seemed for the first time to become aware of the ship and the men. It stopped chewing and looked at them. Then it made a low growling sound.

It seemed to be saying, *"Errrrr!"*

Chane looked it back in the eye.

Again it said, *"Errrrr!"*

Chane suddenly uttered a tremendous roar and ran forward toward the creature, flailing his arms wildly.

The animal dropped the root and scuttled frantically away, and Chane stopped running, and laughed and laughed.

"Chane, you damn crazy fool! It could have been dangerous!" stormed Van Fossan.

"What the devil is going on out here?" demanded Dilullo's voice in the dusk. He had come out of the ship.

Van Fossan explained. Dilullo grunted. "If standing watch is that much fun we'll cut short your turn, Chane. Come on in and sweat with us."

Chane followed him in. In the main bunkroom, under the lights, Bollard and Kimmel and Milner sat around the table.

"Sit down," Dilullo said. "We're trying to decide how to tackle this thing."

"And so of course we need the advice of our newest Merc," said Bollard.

Dilullo told him, "Chane was the one who spotted that code-signal and the only one who knows which building it is. He ought to hear this."

Bollard shrugged, but shut up.

Dilullo told Chane, "We figure that Randall Ashton, or at least some of his party, are prisoners in that building. They saw an Earth-type ship land—you can't mistake our ships with their eyebrow bridges—and they tried to tell us they were there. If Ashton's in there, we've got to get him out. If he's not there, someone is there who should know where Ashton is."

Chane nodded.

Kimmel broke in, saying quickly, "And of course we can't risk landing the ship there again. They'll be expecting that; they'll be all set for us and they'll hit our ship with everything they've got."

He closed his eyes, as though the wrecking of his beloved vessel was too horrible to contemplate.

"So," Dilullo patiently continued, "we're not going to land the ship on Arkuu. We'll swing over and drop the skitter-flier well outside the city, by night. In the flier will be a small party of us. We'll try to get the Ashton people in that building out of there. If we do, we'll call the ship to come back and pick us up outside the city."

Chane nodded again but said nothing. He was not being asked his opinion of the plan, and did not venture to give it.

"I'll lead the landing party," Dilullo told him. "I think Bollard and Milner and Janssen too . . . and you, Chane."

"Of course," said Bollard. "How could we leave out the heroic Chane—the man who nearly got us scragged on Kharali by his playfulness, the man who on Vhol was off boating with a pretty girl while we sat and sweated it out under the gun . . ."

". . . and also," Dilullo added, "the man who can identify the building we have to reach."

"Oh, all right," said Bollard. "But don't you think our party will be a mite small? Five men, to invade a planet?"

"Fifty would be no better, if they caught us," Dilullo said. "The flier won't carry too many, remember, and we may be bringing back four people with us."

He stood up. "Milner, I want you to help check out the weapons we'll take with us."

Twenty-four Earth hours later, the Merc ship came back to Arkuu. Dilullo had picked a time when the capital city was on the dark side of the planet. But the ship went downward a hundred miles away from the city.

Dilullo went over their maps with Kimmel, marking down a spot for emergency rendezvous in case they could not get a call through. Then he went down to the hold, where the others were ready in their places in the flier.

Janssen, the sandy-haired, stocky Merc who was the best man with a flier, sat at the controls, and Dilullo, Bollard, Chane, and Milner in the sketchy bucket-seats.

They could see nothing, here in the dark hold. It was up to Mattock, in the bridge of the ship, to pick the place and the altitude for the drop. They could hear the hold bulk-heads closing.

Then the big ejection-port in the side of the hold slid open. They got just a glimpse, over Janssen's broad shoulders, of a vista of jungle below, lighted by one of the two moons of Arkuu.

"Now," said Mattock's voice from the intercom.

Janssen's hand slammed down on the ejection button. The flier shot out through the port like a bullet.

Its wings and rotors unfolded automatically as it went out. They bit into the atmosphere, finding it roiled and bumpy from the wake of the ship. Janssen steadied the flier gently and swung it around, only a few thousand feet above the jungle.

"Luck, John," said Kimmel's voice from the communicator.

Janssen set a course and the skitter-flier leaped fast. It went high over the jungle like a humming shadow. It had been especially designed for jobs like this one; it had VTO and a motor so near noiseless as to make no difference.

In less than an hour they glimpsed the lights of the city. There were not many; it was late at night here, the way Dilullo had planned it.

"Get over the east side of that spaceport and then take her down," he told Janssen. And to Chane, "Take the scope. Talk Janssen in to the roof of that building you caught the signal from."

Chane watched through the scope as the flier dropped vertically downward. He finally identified the building, which had a few lighted windows.

He gave Janssen direction. After a moment he added, "There's something else. A man seems to be standing guard on the roof."

"Ah, the bastards," said Bollard. "They must have got suspicious we'd come back."

"Could be the guard is a regular thing," Dilullo said curtly. "Anyway, we have to get him before we go down

50

farther. Hold it, Janssen. Milner, use the heavy duty stunner hooked to the scope. Non-lethal."

Milner gave him a wizened grin and came forward, hauling the weapon that looked like an old-fashioned bazooka. He set it into place on the mount atop the scope in the firing-port, and with quick efficiency clicked the synchronizing links into place. Then he opened the port.

Janssen had slowed their descent. Milner peered through the scope, the white of his one eye visible. He made adjustment of its positioning-wheels, squinted again, then pressed the trigger.

The stunner droned. Milner cut it, then raised his head and gave them another pleased, toothy grin.

"He's out."

"All right, Janssen," said Dilullo. "Go on down."

The flier landed on the roof, quiet as an over-sized dragonfly. Dilullo cracked the cabin door and all of them but Janssen went out of it fast, Milner toting along the heavy-duty stunner.

Dilullo's voice, low but forceful, drove them. The building had several stories, and he split them up, each to search through one of its levels.

They ran down stone stairways, feebly illuminated by occasional glowing bulbs in the walls. Chane had the second highest level; he left the stairway and went down a long, poorly-lit corridor, his stunner in his hand.

The marble blocks of the walls had been beautiful once, but they were cracked and grimed with age. This whole world had an antique, battered look, Chane thought. He wondered again what there could be about it that had made the Varnans, who were afraid of nothing, forbid their raiders coming here.

He opened doors along corridors. Nothing. Dark, musty rooms with nothing in them.

Then he found a door that was locked. As he tried it, he thought that he heard movement inside.

Chane drew a pocket atoflash out, with his left hand. Keeping the stunner ready in his right, he used the flash to cut out the lock.

The door swung open and a girl looked at him from the lighted room beyond.

VII

THIS GIRL WAS NO little slip of a thing. She was nearly as tall as Helmer had been, and had the same kind of pale-gold skin and yellow hair. She too wore a belted jerkin, of silken white material, and she had magnificent arms and legs that the garment showed to full advantage.

Her gray-green eyes stared into Chane's, in complete astonishment. She opened her mouth, and he thought that she was going to shout. He was too close to her to use the stunner without getting a backlash from it. He dropped the atoflash and grabbed her, putting his hand over her mouth.

And he got the surprise of his life. This young woman, for all her delectable curves, was stronger than anything feminine he had met since he left Varna. She nearly threw him headlong before he managed to clamp down a tighter grip on her.

Bollard came loping into the corridor from the stair. In danger, he was quite unlike the fat, sloppy Bollard of relaxed moments. His face was drawn tight and the stunner in his hand was ready.

He saw Chane grappling with the tall Arkuun girl; he lowered his weapon a little and stood staring, in wonder and admiration.

"By God, Chane, I have to hand it to you," he said. "You do find fun wherever you go. I hear something up here and come running to save you, and I find you wrestling with a big beautiful blonde."

"Get John," said Chane. "She was was locked up here; there may be others."

He relaxed his grip a little as he spoke. Next moment he was sorry. The Arkuun girl got her teeth around one of his fingers and bit it to the bone.

Chane did not take his hand off her mouth. He swung her around a little, looking into her blazing eyes, and smiled at her.

"I do like a girl with spirit," he said. Then he drew his hand back and cracked her across the point of the chin.

He only used the flat of his hand but he put some of his Starwolf strength into it. The girl's head jerked back and she went out cold.

Chane lowered her to the floor, where she sat with her back against the wall, looking like a discarded doll. As an afterthought, Chane bent down and crossed the long, beautiful legs at the ankles, and put her hands together in her lap. He looked down at her admiringly, as he sucked his bitten finger.

"Isn't she something?" he said.

Dilullo came hurrying into the corridor, with Milner behind him.

"Two guards down at the entrance . . . we stunned them," he said. "Nothing else. What have you got here?"

Chane told him. Dilullo went along the further doors. There was one other door that was locked.

When Dilullo tried it, they heard an excited voice inside, and then a hammering of hands on the door.

"Stand back," said Dilullo.

With the atoflash, he cut the door open.

A young Earthman with stiffly-upstanding black hair and a high-cheekboned Spanish-Indian face came out. His eyes were wild with excitement.

"You're the Earthmen from that ship?" he cried. "I saw it . . . I tried to signal . . ."

"Hold on," said Dilullo. "You're one of Ashton's party?"

"Martin Garcia. It's been weeks ... months ..."

Dilullo interrupted. "Where are the others?"

"Caird's dead," said Garcia, making an effort to calm down. "Died here more than a week ago. Killed? No, he wasn't killed. He caught a bug, seemed to get weaker and weaker. I stayed with him when Ashton and McGoun and the others left."

"Where's Randall Ashton now?" demanded Dilullo.

Garcia spread his hands. "My God, I don't know. He and McGoun got away with the ship and crew, weeks ago. They thought they could find the Free-Faring. The Arkuuns here had forbidden us to look for it, but they went anyway. The Open-Worlders helped them get their ship away. I stayed because Caird looked so bad."

"John, there's no time now for life stories," said Bollard. "If Ashton isn't here, let's go, and get the facts out of this chap later on."

Garcia had caught sight of the girl sitting with her hands in her lap further along the corridor.

"Vreya ... did you kill her?" he exclaimed.

"She's only unconscious," said Bollard. "Who is she, anyway?"

"She was one of the Open-Worlders who helped Ashton get away," said Garcia. "She can talk galacto, and they used her as a secret contact. But Helmer's men caught her and locked her up here like me."

"Would she know where Randall Ashton and the others have gone?" demanded Dilullo.

"I don't know," said Garcia. "I think so."

"We'll take her along with us," Dilullo said decisively. "Now out of here on the double!"

Chane picked up the unconscious girl effortlessly, and they hurried back to the roof. When Janssen, in the flier, saw the long golden legs dangling from Chane's arms, he uttered a low whistle of appreciation.

"Well, you found something, anyway."

"Save the humor," said Dilullo. "Get us out of here—back the way we came. And move!"

The flier went up and away from there, and started arrowing back out across the moonlit jungle. Garcia, in a bucket-seat beside Dilullo, talked rapidly but not incoherently. He had got over his first excitement.

"We were there for nearly two months, the four of us," he said. "In Yarr, the city back there. Randall kept trying to find out from the Arkuuns about the Free-Faring, but their officials wouldn't tell us a thing and kept demanding that we leave. Then the Open-Worlders made secret contact with Randall."

Garcia went on. "The Open-Worlders are Arkuuns who dissent from the rule of keeping the Closed Worlds closed. They want to open the system to interstellar trade. She's one of them."

He nodded toward the girl Vreya. Chane had dropped her into a seat and buckled its strap across her, but she was still unconscious.

"Why would these dissidents want to help Ashton get away to find this—what did you call it?—the Free-Faring? I take it that's the mysterious thing he was after."

"Yes." Garcia shrugged. "They said it was because they wanted him to bring them weapons later on, for a coup. They'd help him find the Free-Faring if he'd promise the weapons."

Bollard grunted, but made no comment. Garcia added, "Anyway, they helped Ashton and Sattargh and McGoun and the crew make a break for the ship and get away. One of them went along, but Vreya, was caught. Caird was sick, dying, so I wouldn't go."

Dilullo made a sound of disgust. "So Randall Ashton not only had to come to the Closed Worlds to chase his interstellar wild goose, he had to get mixed up in local politics and intrigues as well."

He looked sourly at the girl. "Wake her up, Chane."

"With pleasure," said Chane.

He kneaded the nerve centers in the back of the girl's neck until her eyes fluttered open. She looked around the plane, and then looked back at him with a flaming stare.

"You're really too big a girl to bite," he said.

Garcia spoke to her earnestly in galacto. "Vreya, these are friends. They come from Earth looking for Randall Ashton."

Vreya's cool gray-green eyes measured them. Then she asked, "Did you bring a big force of ships?"

Dilullo shook his head. "One small ship. A couple of dozen men."

The Arkuun girl looked disappointed. "What can you expect to accomplish with no more force than that?"

"We didn't come here to interfere in Arkuun politics," said Dilullo pointedly. "We just came to get a few men and take them back to Earth."

Chane, watching the girl's profile, guessed that she was thinking rapidly, trying to evaluate this new factor in the situation. She was, he thought, no fool. With that magnificent body and all that strength she didn't really need a keen mind, but he thought she had one.

Dilullo interrupted her thinking. "Where's Randall Ashton?"

She shook her bright head. "I don't know."

"Why don't you know? You were one of the Arkuun party who got Ashton and the others out of Yarr. Your party helped him to escape so he could find this thing, this . . ."

"Free-Faring," said Garcia.

"You must know where he was going, to find this thing," said Dilullo.

"But I don't," said Vreya. "The Free-Faring has been lost, hidden, for a long time. One of the men with Ashton, the man named McGoun, thought he knew where it could be found. We helped him escape, but I was caught."

Dilullo stared at her. "What is this thing he's looking for, anyway—this Free-Faring?"

Vreya remained silent, but a light came briefly into her eyes and then was gone. Dilullo turned to Garcia. "You must know—you came all the way out here to the Closed Worlds to look for it."

Garcia looked uncomfortalble. "Ashton didn't tell us all that McGoun told him. Of course, it's been a legend for a long time but the stories are contradictory."

"Come off it," said Dilullo. "You must know *something* of what the thing is supposed to be."

Garcia got a dogged look on his face. "It's supposed to be something by which a man can go anywhere in the universe in a minute."

They stared, and then Chane uttered a low laugh. "Just like that?" he said. "Convenient."

"For God's sake!" cried Dilullo. "You mean you followed Ashton all the way to Allubane for a myth as crazy as that?"

Vreya spoke, her face flushed, her eyes bright. "It is no myth." This time she did not try to conceal the intensity of her interest. "It existed. It may still exist."

Dilullo could only shake his head. Janssen spoke from the control-chair of the flier, turning his head toward them.

"I'd just like to remind you, John, that it'll soon be daylight and that the Arkuuns have fliers and will be looking for us."

Dilullo frowned. Then he said, "No use calling the ship back till we find Ashton or some clear lead to him. We'll set down for a while."

"Set down?" exclaimed Janssen. He motioned toward the dense jungle underneath them, brightly illumined now that the second moon had climbed into the sky. "There isn't an opening in that stuff big enough for a fly to set down!"

"We passed over some ruined cities," Dilullo said. "Set down in one of those."

Janssen grunted, and changed the course of the flier. Vreya had not understood their English, but when she saw the white gleam of ruins far ahead, she understood.

"I have to warn you," she said in galacto, "that there are highly dangerous life-forms in the jungles."

"I haven't a doubt of it," said Dilullo, looking down distastefully at the moonlit expanse. "Nevertheless, we have to hole up somewhere and camouflage the flier and wait till the search for us dies down."

"And then what?" asked Bollard.

Dilullo shrugged. "Why, then we go ahead and do the job we were hired for . . . we look for Randall Ashton."

"You always make it sound so simple, John," said Bollard.

"That's because it is," said Dilullo sourly. "Danger and sudden death are always simple things. Take her down, Janssen."

VIII

CHANE WALKED AMID shifting, ever-changing shadows as he went through the towering ruins. The two moons were both up, and they struck down a glow of tarnished silver light that made the white walls and buttresses and statues as unreal as a dream. The soft light was kind to the ruins, and it was not too apparent where a roof had fallen in or a wall had collapsed.

The breeze was warm and sluggish, and heavy with the dry-rot smell of the jungle. There were little sounds of small animals and birds that lived in the ruins, but nothing else. Under his feet the stone blocks were here and there thrust askew by roots, but the old builders had worked well and the streets were still streets.

"Now what does this place remind me of?" Chane asked himself.

Then he remembered. It had been two years ago, when the Starwolves had raided the Pleiades. Chane had been one of them, and Nimurun had been the leader; he had always been reckless, even for a Varnan. He had got their squadron boxed and it had looked like a fight at long odds.

But they had found a hidey-hole, an uninhabited, lifeless little planet that had been blasted by some past war. Its metal buildings that remained were twisted and misshapen like the tortured ghosts of buildings. For three days and nights they had lain hidden and listened to the wind moan through those wrecked buildings, but they had not been found. Eventually they had got safely out of the Pleiades.

Chane did not like ruined cities. He liked cities that were bustling with life and full of costly and desirable things that could be looted.

He grinned. *That's Starwolf thinking,* he told himself. *You must keep remembering that you're a good honest Merc now.*

They had landed here less than an hour ago. A camouflage net had been drawn quickly over the flier, and none too soon, for presently other fliers from the direction of Yarr had swung over the ruins, circling and circling and then gone on again. That the hunt for them was on, was quite obvious.

Then Janssen got the jitters. He swore that he glimpsed men flitting around in the jungle beyond the ruins, spying on them. Dilullo had patiently pointed out that it was quite impossible that any Arkuuns could have got here this soon. Janssen persisted in his assertion.

"I'll go out and have a look around," Chane had volunteered. He was already bored with sitting on his hunkers under the net.

"No," said Dilullo. "If there are any of them out there, we'll know it it soon enough."

"Ah, let him go, John," said Bollard. "He's young blood, he's restless; can't you see that? He's not like us poor old crocks."

Dilullo shrugged. "Okay, Chane, take a look and see what Janssen's spooks are."

Chane nodded, and told Bollard, "I'll do my best to come back safely. For your sake."

Bollard guffawed and said that Chane was going to be the death of him one of these days as Chane had left them.

In the ruins, there was apparently nobody at all. But there was life of some kind out in the jungle. He paused once, hearing a sound, and caught the echoes of a faraway cry, long, falling inflections that were wordless yet sounded as though they might have come from a human throat.

There was no sharp line of demarcation between city and jungle. Chane gradually passed into a zone where there was more vegetation than ruins, and then it came to be thick jungle with only an occasional bulk of carved stones here and there amid the foliage.

He had been in many forests on many worlds. It was a favorite Starwolf tactic to land by night in such places and then make their spring from that cover, upon their target. Chane knew how to move silently, to slip always from one shadow to another, to bring his foot down softly. He stopped from time to time to listen, but there were only the small cheepings and rustlings normal to any jungle.

He listened for a repetition of that weird far away call but he did not hear it again.

No one, he thought. *Janssen was just seeing things.*

Then an odd thing happened. The skin between his shoulders seemed to tighten, and the short hairs on the back of his neck seemed to rise.

Danger. And near . . .

The Starwolves had no sixth sense, but they had trained the five they had to an utter keenness. Something—some smell, or almost inaudible sound—had reached and warned him.

Chane silently whirled around. He thought that he just glimpsed a white something vanish behind one of the giant trees.

He went there, his stunner in his hand.

Nothing.

There was the faintest of rustles and he spun around fast again, and thought he glimpsed another vague white shape flit from sight.

With appalling suddenness, the voice he had heard from far away sounded loudly from close by. It was not a human voice, and it spoke no words. It laughed, a kind of sobbing, shivery laughter.

Then the unhuman sound cut off sharply, and there was silence again.

Chane waited, his face dark and dangerous in a bar of the shifting moonlight. They were around him and they thought they had him, and so they were laughing.

He faced back toward the ruined city. He was not afraid, but he had all a Varnan's cunning caution. This world and what it might contain were new to him; he must go carefully.

He took a half dozen steps and then something came out of the brush ahead of him.

He thought at first that it was a man, and then as the moonlight shifted slightly he saw that it was manlike but not human. It had arms and legs and a body and a head. It wore no clothing, and was apparently sexless. It came slowly toward him and he saw a face that had softly glowing big eyes, no nose at all—just a blank space where the nose should be—and a nauseatingly pretty little mouth.

Chane triggered the stunner, aiming directly at the thing. Nothing happened at all, except that the thing uttered that sobbing laugh again.

He notched the stunner to lethal and fired again.

Again, nothing happened.

He knew then that the stunner, designed to paralyze the nervous system of a mammalian or near-mammalian creature, was useless.

A sudden thought occurred to him. The thing had been a little too obvious about coming out and holding his attention. There could be another one behind him . . .

Chane started to turn but did not complete the movement. A living weight landed on his back, and smooth cold arms went around his throat. The grip tightened, swiftly choking him.

All right, thought Chane. *But you haven't caught a man: you've caught a Starwolf.*

He put all his Varnan strength into a great surge of arms and shoulders to break the grip.

It did not break. He realized, even as he began to gasp for air, that he had finally met something as strong as he was. Perhaps stronger.

That appalling knowledge triggered a wild revulsion in Chane's mind. He stopped trying to break the choking grip. He flexed his knees and sprang, hurling himself and the thing upon his back with him, away from there.

He turned in mid-air and when they hit the ground the white shape on his back hit underneath him. The impact jarred its hold, not much, but enough to weaken it. Chane burst free.

The white man-thing was up quicker than a cat, coming at him and making a hideous little mewing sound. Chane's hand flashed and hit its neck. The neck should have broken but it did not. It was like hitting pure gristle and muscle without a bone.

He pretended he was going to strike again, but it was his foot that flashed this time and his boot caught the thing in the stomach. It was knocked back into the brush.

Chane whirled around just in time. The one that had been laughing was only a few feet from him, the delicately-fingered white hands reaching for him.

He struck and struck. He was sweating and scared now, the more so because he thought he could hear the light running steps of a third thing coming.

Chane suddenly sprang and ran. He could not face two of these creatures—it was doubtful if he could even match one. Three, if there were three, would certainly kill him.

He went through the brush with all the furious speed of which his body was capable. And he could not lose the things. They flitted almost beside him, lithe and swift as white panthers, seeking to draw ahead of him and cut off his escape.

He was among the marble ruins and they were about

to block his way, when he heard yelling voices, and then the hiss and flash and searing crack of a portable laser letting go.

The white ones went away into the brush so fast that he hardly saw them go, and then he saw Dilullo coming through the ruins with Janssen and with Milner, the latter holding one of the portable lasers in his hands.

"We heard you threshing around out there," said Dilullo. "Who the devil were they?"

"Not who—what," said Chane. He was more shaken than he had been for a long time. "They aren't people. I don't know what they are, but it's something pretty nasty." He added, for Dilullo's especial benefit, "They almost got me." His voice had a note of dismayed incredulity. Dilullo got the warning.

They went back to where the flier hid under its camouflage net. The others were there, Bollard and Garcia and the girl Vreya.

Chane described what he had met out in the jungle. When he had finished, Vreya said, "The Nanes."

"The what?"

"The word *Nane*, in our language, means 'not a man'. They're not too bright, but they're deadly."

"You didn't mention them, that I recall," Dilullo said to her, in an edged voice.

Vreya turned toward him. "I told you there was dangerous life in the jungles. What do you expect me to do—mother you?"

Bollard exploded into laughter, and Chane grinned. Dilullo looked angrily at them. "What kind of evolution could produce things like that?"

Vreya looked around at the tall ruins that towered into the silver light. "There were great scientists in these cities in the old days. It was they who created the Free-Faring. And it is said that they also created the Nanes. The creatures don't breed. But on the other hand they were made to be practically immortal, and there are still some of them in the jungles."

Milner said in a whining voice, "A real ugly world we've come to, I think. I don't like it."

"Nobody," said Dilullo, "has ever paid Mercs big money to go somewhere and have a good time. Go to sleep. Chane, you've kept us all up with your prowling. You can stand first watch."

Chane nodded, and took the portable laser from Milner. The others went and got into their sleeping bags and stretched out.

The two moons wheeled across the starry sky, the distance between them getting bigger all the time and the forked shadows more bizarre. From far out in the jungle came a sobbing cry.

Chane smiled. "No, my friend," he muttered. "Not again."

After a while he heard movement, and turned. Vreya had got out of the sleeping bag they had given her. She walked out to where Chane stood guard amid a tumbled mass of giant blocks, and sat down on one of the blocks.

Chane watched her, admiring her beautiful arms and legs. They were all silver now in the tarnished light.

"This place depresses me," she told him.

He shrugged. "I'll admit I've seen more amusing places myself."

She looked at him somberly. "It doesn't mean anything to you. You've just come here; it's only another strange world to you, and you'll soon go away again. But to us . . ."

She was silent for a time, and then said, "This was a great trading city, once. There was a big starport north of here. Ships went out and traded with star-worlds far up what you call the Perseus Arm. And others went farther. The people of Arkuu were starfarers for generations. Now we live in dust and memories on two little planets, and there are no more stars for us at all."

Her voice took on a note of passion. "Because of old,

superstitious fears, we have become the Closed Worlds. No one must come to Allubane, and we must not go away from it. But some of us work to lift that senseless ban, and because of it we are called plotters and traitors by men like Helmer, who follow blind dogmas."

Chane felt a strong sympathy. He had lived too long as a Starwolf not to sympathize with anyone barred from roving the starways.

"Perhaps the time has come when the Closed Worlds will be open again," he said.

She said nothing to that, but looked away at the ruined towers that had been strong and joyous once.

Chane felt a surge of warmth toward her. He went to where she sat and bent over her.

Her shapely knee came up and cracked his chin. He saw stars as he staggered back.

He shook his head to clear it. She was looking at him with contemptuous self-assurance. Chane suddenly leaped and grabbed her. His hand went over her mouth as it had done the other time.

She struggled with the strength of a tigress. But Chane used all his iron force and held her.

"Now," he whispered in her ear, "I can do just what I want to do."

Again she tried to break free, but the Starwolf strength held her. "And what I want to do," Chane whispered, "is . . . tell you that I like you."

He gave her a great smacking kiss on the cheek and then let her go and stepped back. And at the mingled rage and astonishment on her face, he began to laugh.

Vreya looked at him, her hands clenched into fists, and then her face softened and she laughed also.

She said in a low voice, "Raul will be very angry with me for this."

And, still laughing, she came up close to Chane and kissed him on the mouth.

67

IX

DILULLO WOKE UP IN the morning with pains in his shoulders and his rump. He had slept in the aisle of the flier instead of out in the open like the others. He had met and faced many strange forms of life on many worlds, but one thing he could never get used to was insects. The thought of them crawling over his face had made him prefer the hard floor to a sleeping bag outside.

He felt rusty and mean. He got a drink of water and brushed his teeth, and then went outside. The topaz sun was well up over the horizon, throwing a flood of yellow light over everything. He went out from under the camouflage net, toward the brushy ruins a little distance away.

As he went he passed the girl Vreya, lying in her sleeping bag, her yellow hair rumpled and her face in the repose of slumber looking childish and cherubic. He gazed down at her with an oddly fatherly feeling.

Probably a no-good wench, he thought, *and doubtless trying to use us all for her own purposes. But a nice-looking girl.*

He went on and met Janssen, who had taken over the second watch. Janssen yawned and said that nothing had happened.

When Dilullo returned he went into the flier and came back out with one of the documents that James Ashton had given him. It was a map of Arkuu—not a very good map, since the Closed Worlds had forcefully discouraged topographical surveys—but the only one he had.

He sat down on the shady side of the flier with his back against a wheel and frowned at the map. After a minute, he looked around. Nobody was stirring. Dilullo reached into the pocket of his coverall and brought out a small case. He took from it a pair of spectacles and put them on and then re-examined the map.

A few minutes later, a shadow fell across him. He looked up quickly. It was Chane, regarding him with interest.

Dilullo gave him a hard, challenging stare. He meant it to say, "Yes, I wear spectacles to read when no one's around, and you had better keep your mouth shut about it."

But the stare was wasted. Chane was pure brass. He looked down at Dilullo and said,

"I never saw those before. Eyes getting a little weak, eh?"

Dilullo snarled. "Is that any of your business?"

Chane started laughing. He said, "John, let me tell you something. You're the smartest among us, and you could probably beat up any one of us, except me, of course."

"Of course," said Dilullo, between his teeth.

"Stop worrying about getting old," Chane continued. "All around, you're the best man—except me, of course . . ."

"Of course," said Diulllo, but he had a bleak grin on his face now.

He took the spectacles off and put them away. "All right, break out some rations for breakfast. And wake up your girl friend. I want a serious talk with her."

Chane looked puzzled. "My girl friend?"

Dilullo said, "Look, my eyes may be a little weak at reading, but I generally know what's going on around me. Get her."

When Vreya came, Dilullo motioned to her to sit down, and then spoke to her in galacto.

"We brought you along because we thought you might be able to tell us where Ashton went. But you're not a prisoner. If you want to go back, you can stay here and signal the next flier that comes over looking for us."

"Go back to being locked up?" said Vreya. "No, I don't want to go back."

"I take it, then," said Dilullo, "you want to join your friend who went with Ashton—what was his name?"

"Raul," she said. "He's the leader of our party. The Open-Worlders, they call us, because we want the freedom of the stars again." She added bitterly, "Helmer calls us other things, like conspirators and traitors."

"All right, stay with us and guide us to where Ashton and Raul and the others went," said Dilullo.

Vreya shook her head. "It's not that easy. All I know is the general area they were going to. It's where the legends have always said the Free-Faring was hidden, but it's a big area."

"How big? Show me, on the map."

Vreya's fine eyes studied the map intently. Dilullo handed her a pencil, and with it she drew a large irregular circle in the north.

"Somewhere in there," she said.

Dilullo looked, and his face grew long. "That's the devil and all of a big area. And mountains, too."

"The highest on Arkuu," she said. "There are valleys of jungle between them."

"Oh, fine," he muttered. "We can't search an area like that from the air." He frowned, thinking. Then he said, "You told me that this area is where legends put the Free-Faring. I take it Helmer and his bunch would know the legends, too?"

She nodded. "Yes; he went with fliers to look for Raul and Ashton and the rest, but it's as you said: you can't comb an area like that from the air."

"Then," said Dilullo, "Helmer would know that we're heading there, too, since he knows we're out to find Ashton." He shook his head. "That spells trouble."

The others were awake. Janssen came in from guard duty and they sat around in a circle under the net, eating their breakfast rations.

When they had finished them, Dilullo began an informal council of war. He had found long ago that Mercs would do almost anything you asked them, if they knew beforehand what they were into, and what the reasons were. You could not order them around high-handedly; you had to lay it out to them.

He laid it out to them. Nobody said anything for a little while. Then Bollard, who was always pessimistic when he was separated from the supply of beer in the ship, shook his head.

"So we go up to this mountain area," he said. "What do we do there? I mean, if Helmer and the other Arkuuns couldn't find Ashton and his bunch when it's their world, how can we?"

"We've got a few gadgets the Arkuuns don't seem to have," Dilullo pointed out. "Like metal-locators of considerable accuracy. If Ashton's ship set down somewhere up there, we should be able to find it and pick up the trail from there."

They thought about that and did not seem very enthusiastic, but nobody objected. They knew it was risky, but being a Merc was a risky business.

"Janssen," said Dilullo.

"Yes?"

"You got a look at the Arkuun fliers that first time we landed at the spaceport. What do you think of them, compared to ours?"

Janssen was a nut about fliers. He considered starships a way of making a living, but dull. Flying a winged craft in atmosphere really excited him.

He said, "They really looked pretty good, John. But a little old-fashioned. They don't have VTO, I don't think they have the speed we have, and I doubt if they have the range."

Vreya, who had been getting increasingly bored with a conversation she did not understand, demanded to know what all this was about. Chane told her, in galacto.

"Of course our fliers are old-fashioned," she said bitterly. "We do not go out to the stars any more; we do not know what progress is being made on other worlds. We do not know what goes on in the galaxy. My clothes are the same that Arkuun women have worn for generations."

They looked at her, at the short jerkin and her golden arms and legs, and all of them except Dilullo and Garcia uttered a unanimous wolf-whistle.

"Knock it off," said Dilullo. He added, poker-faced, "Chane, I appoint you to chaperone this friendless girl and protect her from these Casanovas."

Chane goggled and said, "Huh?" and Dilullo felt pleased with himself, thinking, *That's the first time I ever took Chane by surprise.*

He turned to the others. "As I've told you, I've got an idea that Helmer, or some of Helmer's men, will be up in that area waiting for us. What I want to know first is, could we slip up by night and land in the center of that area. Janssen?"

Janssen frowned, but after a moment he reluctantly shook his head. "I'd love to try it, for the heck of it. But landing by moonlight in the midst of high mountains, with no beacons and God knows what downdrafts—I have to tell you, John, it'd be suicide."

Dilullo nodded. "Okay, I'll take your word for it. So we go by daylight and run our chances. Milner?"

"Yes?"

"You fit one of the heavy lasers to the firing port of the plane. I've an idea we may want it."

Milner's weazened face cracked in a grin. "Figure to blast them out of the sky if they get in our way, eh?"

Dilullo said levelly, "You are a bloody-minded so-and-so. We are not going to kill anyone unless we have to, to save our own necks. Remember, this is the Arkuuns' world, and not ours. I don't want any big sweat with them; I just want to get Randall Ashton and go. If we meet fliers you'll try to disable them, nothing more."

Milner went sulkily off to mount the laser.

An hour later they had the camouflage net rolled up and stored inside the flier, and Janssen took them up out of the ruins into the lemon-colored glare of Allubane.

Dilullo, looking down from his seat, saw something flash out of the jungle and then, for a moment, he saw a face looking up at him, a noseless white face with glowing eyes and a horrible little mouth. It flashed out of sight as Janssen threw in the horizontal drive.

Dilullo thought, *No wonder Chane was shaken up last night, if that's what he met. Not only hideous, but dangerous as well. Strong . . . too strong even for a Varnan.*

He looked at Chane, sitting beside Vreya and talking to her in a low voice, and thought, *I wish I were young and carefree like that again.* And then he thought, *But I never was as carefree as Chane; nobody ever was, except a Starwolf.*

Their flier went north and north for hours. Endless red jungle, starred here and there by old white ruins. A yellow river seemed to run north-south and was a big, tawny flood.

It seemed as though the crimson jungle would go on forever. But finally, as Allubane was declining toward the horizon, Janssen spoke from where he handled the controls.

"John."

Dilullo went up and looked over his shoulder. Far ahead, dark mountains shouldered the yellow sky.

"They're plenty high," he said.

"Not the mountains," Janssen said. "This side of them, at about twelve o'clock."

Dilullo peered. His far sight was pretty good, and presently he saw the small black specks against the lemon sky, getting rapidly bigger.

"Fliers," he said dismally. "I was afraid of that." He turned around and yelled, "Milner!"

Milner, who had been looking singularly unlovely as he slept with his mouth open, came bounding out of his seat.

"Man that laser," said Dilullo. "Remember what I told you— no killing if we can help it. Aim at their tail sections."

Milner shrugged. "You show me a nice safe way to shoot people out of the sky without hurting them, I'll do it."

Dilullo gave him the special smile that he reserved for people who were being difficult. "Try to, Milner," he said.

Milner had seen that smile before; he muttered, "Oh, all right," and went to the firing-port.

"Buckle in," Dilullo told Chane and the others. "I think we're in for a little rough flying."

The three Arkuun fliers came rushing at them. Janssen, moving swiftly, flipped the controls and their own flier stood on its tail. Something flashed by and there was an explosion well behind them.

"Missiles," said Janssen. "Pretty close, too."

"Close with them," said Dilullo. "Be ready with that laser, Milner."

Janssen did a swift loop and sent the flier rushing forward again. The three Arkuun craft, fast but not so maneuverable, tried to take evasive action, but Janssen brought the flier down on them from a higher altitude.

"Look, I'm one of those old pilots back in the Twentieth Century's World War One that I read about!" said Janssen happily. "Dogfights in a Spad, yet! *Eh-eh-eh-eh-eh!*" And he made a sound like a machine-gun going off.

"For God's sake, why did I have to go to the stars with a comedian!" said Dilullo.

Then the three Arkuun fliers rushed up at them.

X

THE LASER FLASHED and cracked. Milner was aiming for the leading flier.

He missed. Janssen threw the skitter-flier around in a fast curve and then came back toward the other fliers again.

"How many chances do you need to hit something?" he said, without turning his head.

Milner, who was an expert with the laser and rarely missed, said something so unprintable that it made Dilullo glad that Vreya couldn't understand it.

Missiles zipped past them, but far wide. The Arkuuns veered their course, but a shade too late. Milner let go with the laser again, slicing through the tail of the leading flier.

Chane sat and watched the flier go fluttering down. He felt an enormous interest in this kind of fighting, which was new to him. The Starwolves rarely used air-fliers in fighting; they usually didn't have the time to haul them out and get going with them, when they raided a world.

He saw that the damaged flier was heading toward the only possible landing place in the thick jungle—the wide, tawny river that ran away southward. The pilot made it; he saw the flier smack the water and its two occupants scrambling out of it. Chane grinned. Dilullo, with his prejudice against killing, would be pleased.

Vreya, beside him, was not looking out now. She was looking at Chane in surprise and wonder.

She started to say something but at that moment Janssen threw the skitter-flier around in a roll-over and turn that threw them hard against their belts.

The Arkuuns seemed momentarily bewildered by the unexpected maneuver. Milner triggered the laser, aiming at the nearest of the two fliers. He missed again, just grazing and cutting a few inches off the wing-tip of the Arkuun craft.

Milner's profanity this time was unspeakable. He swung the laser around.

"Hold it," said Dilullo. "They're sheering off."

The Arkuun fliers, their occupants apparently losing nerve, were now racing away toward the east.

"Let them go," said Dilullo.

He unfolded the map on his knees and squinted at it. "There's a city named Anavan marked, not too far to the east," he said. "They'll soon be back with more fliers, so we don't have unlimited time. Janssen, you set up a sweep pattern. Bollard can run the locator."

Chane found Vreya still studying him with a wondering look. "You were amused when we were in danger," she said. "You were smiling."

Chane shook his head. "Just covering up my nervousness, that's all."

"I don't think so," said Vreya. "You're different from these others. Last night while you were out in the jungle, that man"—she nodded her head toward Milner—"caught me away from the others. I broke his hold easily and hit him in the face. He had nothing like your strength."

Chane shrugged. "My strength just comes from regular exercises and leading a moral life."

Vreya's gray-green eyes became mocking. "When did you start leading it—early this morning?"

Bollard had taken the co-pilot seat. In front of it were the instruments of the metal-locator, along with the radio-active-matter detector, the atmosphere analyzer, and all the other complex instruments you needed if you meant to use a flier on alien worlds. The locator was designed to throw a broad fan of force, analogous to radar but responsive only to metal.

"Garcia says that Ashton's ship is a Class Four, crew of eight," Dilullo said. "Set it so it won't get echo from anything much smaller than that."

Bollard grunted, and bent to adjust the controls on the face of the instrument. Finally he said, "Okay."

Dilullo nodded to Janssen, who started the skitter-flier on an east-west course.

Chane said, "Vreya."

"Yes?"

"You don't want us to find Randall Ashton, do you?"

Her eyes went cold. "Why wouldn't I?"

"Because," Chane said, "I think it was you and your Open-Worlders who wanted him lost in the first place. Why should you people come and get Ashton free, so he could go off into the wilderness searching for the Free-Faring?"

"I told you," she said. "We offered that in exchange for weapons he would bring us later . . ."

"That's a thin explanation," said Chane. "I think you wanted Ashton lost—good and lost—because you'd found out he was a very rich and very important man back on Earth. You people figured there'd be an expedition of some kind come cracking into the Closed Worlds to find him, and that's what you wanted."

Her face became stormy and he thought for a moment that she was going to hit him.

"Now I want to tell you something about John," said Chane. "he never gives up. He won't give up now. He'll keep searching with the locator for Ashton's ship until he finds it. Or until Helmer gets a report from those two fliers, and comes here with a bigger squadron to shoot us out of the sky. Helmer will do that, won't he?"

"Yes," she said bitterly. "He and his fanatics who follow

old superstitions and dogmas will kill, if necessary, to keep the Closed Worlds closed."

"Janssen and Milner are pretty good," said Chane. "But I don't think they can stand off a squadron."

"You're trying to frighten me," she accused.

Chane grinned. "I don't think you frighten very easily, lovely. But I believe you've miscalculated. You think John will give up searching before Helmer comes. I'm telling you he won't."

Doubt replaced the anger in her eyes. Chane added, "If you know anything that'll get us down from this sitting-duck position, now is the time to tell it."

She looked again at Dilullo, standing behind Bollard, and the bleak, grim look in his harsh-boned face seem finally to convince her.

"All right," she said.

Chane said to Dilullo, "Vreya has remembered something that might help us find the ship."

"Ah-huh," said Dilullo. "I kind of thought she might."

Chane decided that while Dilullo might not have the cunning of a Starwolf, he was pretty good at running a bluff.

Vreya studied the map again and then made a pencil-mark on it. "There is the place where they were going to land the ship. Then they would use a small flier to begin searching for the Free-Faring."

Chane thought, *And Ashton would be off on a wild-goose chase that would keep him lost till it made big trouble for the Closed Worlds. Yes.*

Dilullo took the map to Janssen and presently the skitter-flier started going almost due north, at its highest speed.

Vreya turned her face pointedly away from Chane. He shrugged, closed his eyes, and went to sleep.

He woke up to find the skitter-flier was still humming quietly along. Most of the others were sleeping. Chane knew that it was hours later, for the yellow flare of Allubane was much farther down the sky.

He went forward and looked over Janssen's shoulders.

"Rugged," said Janssen. "Real rugged."

Ahead of them, a stupendous range of dark mountains shouldered up against the sky. Beyond it, they could see isolated peaks of still other ranges, like great fangs.

"It's a mess," said Janssen. "And a valley in that mess is where we're heading. Wish me luck, Chane."

"Luck," said Chane, and went back to his chair.

Vreya was sleeping like the others, and he thought it wisest to let her sleep.

A little later, Dilullo woke up, yawning and stretching. "How long now?" he asked Janssen.

"Half an hour . . . maybe a little more," said Janssen.

Dilullo came fully awake. He went forward and bent over the pilot's shoulder.

"All right," he said. "It's time we started getting clever. We have to assume the Arkuuns have pretty good radar. The way they smacked our ship out in space would indicate that."

"So?"

"So change course. Don't go toward the spot behind the range we're actually heading for. Cross the range a long way west of that spot, come down behind the range and then fly back east under cover so they can't radar us."

Janssen turned around and looked at him. "Did you ever fly one of these things much, John?"

"I can handle one if I have to," said Dilullo. "I never made a profession out of it."

"Be glad of that," said Janssen. "You won't be worrying so much when I carry out that order of yours."

The skitter-flier went over the range, heading obliquely in a northwest direction now. Chane looked down at the dark, bare humps of the mountains. Already the forested valleys between them were starting to fill with dusk.

Janssen swung them down behind the range, then started eastward. It was dizzying flying, for the mountains towered up all around them, stark against the lemonish glare of the setting sun. The change of direction woke the other Mercs. Bollard lamented audibly that he had no beer. The others looked yawny and stupid. A lot of the time, Chane thought, a Merc looked and felt that way.

"Just up ahead," said Janssen finally. "That valley."

They were approaching a place where a forested valley angled off northeastward into the mountains.

"All right," said Dilullo to Bollard, and Bollard turned the locator on again.

The skitter-flier went up the angling valley at no more than a thousand feet above the treetops.

"Take her up a bit," said Bollard. "I can't sweep the whole valley this low."

Janssen took the flier up. In no more than ten minutes, Bollard exclaimed, "Got it." He added, "I think."

They peered down. Chane could see nothing but a forest of incredibly huge and lofty trees. But at one point in the crimson sea of foliage, there was a break. It was a clearing where there appeared to have been a fire in recent years, but there was nothing much in the clearing.

"It could be it," said Dilullo. "They could have landed in that clearing and then used the ship's power to kick it back under the trees. Those trees are far enough apart, and a Class Four is a small enough ship, to make it possible."

He made a quick decision. "Take us down there, Janssen."

Janssen circled around and came back and then dropped them down on VTO drive. The skitter-flier came to rest in the clearing.

They went out of the flier and looked around in the twilight. From the air, the clearing had looked untouched. But once on the ground, Chane saw instantly where a small ship had landed, and had then been kicked beneath the gigantic trees. The scars in the ground had been camouflaged with brush and litter, but you could see them clearly enough when you stood on the ground.

Dilullo started following the camouflaged scars in the ground. They passed under the shade of the trees. Only on one or two worlds had Chane ever seen trees so huge. They went hundreds of feet into the air, and they were a thousand feet or more apart, as befitted their mightiness. The twilight under them was deepened almost into darkness.

They had not far to go. A bare few hundred feet ahead, a bulk of metal glinted dully.

"As easy as that," said Chane.

"A little too easy," said Bollard. "Mercs don't get anything this easy."

A few minutes later, Chane decided that Bollard was right. They were nearing the ship when Dilullo stopped and looked down and to one side.

Chane looked that way and saw something white. Bones. Human bones, polished clear by the scavengers or insects of the forest.

"You're an anthropologist, Garcia," said Dilullo. "Take a look."

Garcia went and bent over the bones, and they all waited until he took a look.

"Definitely terrestrial," said Garcia. He looked troubled. "Three Earthmen. But what bothers me is that the skulls of two of them and the arms of one have been torn clean loose from the main skeleton."

"Animals?"

"I don't think so," said Garcia. He added, "None of them is Ashton or McGoun. I know the shape of their skulls."

"A pity," muttered Bollard. "If we could find Ashton's indubitable remains, we could take them and go peacefully home and make a lot of money without any more trouble."

Dilullo said nothing, but led on toward the ship. Outside it, he stopped again. There were more bones. They seemed to be of two men, but they were so mixed up that it was hard to be sure. Not only both skulls but three arms and one leg were torn loose and lying at a little distance.

Chane looked without any emotion as Garcia examined these. He had seen too many men die to be much affected by their remains. Vreya looked tensely on, beside him.

Again, Garcia shook his head. "Two more terrestrial types, but not Ashton or McGoun."

The lock door of the ship yawned wide. It looked dark inside the craft but Dillullo led the way unhesitatingly in.

There was light enough to see the mess. It was a real mess, not just the fact that there were more broken bones in here. The whole interior of the ship was broken up.

Every instrument, every control, seemed to have been shattered or twisted. It was as though a tornado of destruction had raged through the ship, smashing all but its heaviest components.

Chane looked down at the floor where he stood. There was a brown smear there where blood had dried. And there was a print in the smear . . . the print of a toeless foot. He remembered very clearly where he had seen such a toeless foot, only the night before.

Vreya looked down too, and shivered.

"So that was it," she said. "The Nanes."

XI

"Go BACK AND GET two lasers," Dilullo said sharply to Chane. "And tell Janssen to taxi the skitter-flier here."

He did not need to tell Chane to hurry. Chane went at a fast lope back through the deepening dusk. He glanced this way and that as he ran, half expecting to see a white shape slip from behind one of the mighty trunks, but there was nothing. Chane had had a good many fights on more starworlds than he could remember, but he had never fought anything so frightful and repulsive as the white man-things he had met the night before.

He got two of the smaller portable lasers and gave Janssen Dilullo's message. Then Chane ran back, keeping just as wary an eye as before.

Dilullo took one of the lasers and gave Milner the other. "Stand guard outside the lock," he told Milner. "I want the flier covered at all times when Janssen brings it up."

He swung around. "The rest of you get the bones and wreckage out of the ship, so we can spend the night there. You can use hand-lamps inside, but no lights outside the ship."

They got the lamps and went inside. Dilullo angled his light around and then started picking his way over the debris in the corridor that led forward.

"I'm going to look for the ship's log," he said. "Garcia, you come with me."

Chane and Bollard, and Janssen, after he had brought

the flier up, started clearing up the mess. Vreya found and cleared a gimballed chair that had escaped damage, and sat gloomily watching them.

They got the bones and wreckage out of this main compartment and worked back through a couple of the tiny cabins. In one of them, Janssen uttered an exclamation.

"Hey, look at this."

He picked up a bottle of brandy that had miraculously escaped breaking when the contents of a cabinet had been pulled out. He happily opened it, but Bollard interrupted.

"What? Drinking on the job? Hand over that bottle."

Janssen handed it over. "Aw . . ." he began.

"Could be anything in this liquor," said Bollard. "As subleader, it's my responsibility to test it."

He up-ended the bottle and took a mighty drink. "It's okay," he said, wiping his lips. "Have one."

Janssen and Chane each had one, and then they finished clearing the cabin. When Chane went back into the main compartment it was dark, but he could see Vreya sitting with her back to him, looking tensely at the open lock-door.

He slipped noiselessly up behind her and suddenly grabbed her from behind the chair.

Vreya let out a screech and jumped up, and then turned around and spoke with rapidity and fury. In her passion she forgot, and used her own language.

Chane listened in admiration, and when she paused for breath, he said in galacto, "All wasted. I can't speak Arkuun, remember."

"I can give you a translation," she began, but he shook his head. "Don't bother. My sensitive feelings might be hurt."

She told him what he could do about his sensitive feelings, and he went laughing out through the lock to where Milner stood guard in the darkness.

Milner said there was nothing stirring, and Chane went back in to find Dilullo and Garcia coming back from the bridge, their hand-lamps cutting through the gloom.

"What's going on back here?" said Dilullo. "I heard a yell."

"Vreya's a little nervous," said Chane. "You can hardly blame the girl."

Vreya told Chane angrily, "Talk galacto when you're talking about me."

"Might as well," said Dilullo, switching to the lingua-franca. "It'll save repeating to her later. What's that you've got there?"

The latter words were addressed to Janssen, who with Bollard had come from aft.

"Bottle of brandy I salvaged," said Janssen. "I was bringing it to you."

"I'll bet," grunted Dilullo. He took the bottle and offered it to Garcia, who refused, then took a drink from it and set it down on the floor beside him.

"I found the log," he said, and Chane saw that he held a thick book whose plastic cover had been ripped apart and whose leaves were falling out. "It doesn't help us much. This ship got here the first night, they butted it back under the trees for concealment, and next day, Ashton, Raul, Sattargh and McGoun started out in the small skitter-flier they had stored in the hold. Captain and crew were to wait here for them."

"What I figured," said Bollard. "And the Nanes took the crew by surprise and tore them apart."

"Raul would have warned them about the Nanes," Vreya said sharply.

Dilullo nodded. "Probably he did. But if so, they took the warning too lightly. How many of these nasty creatures are there, anyway?"

"Nobody knows, really," said Vreya. "But there are more here in the north than anywhere else on Arkuu. There's a dead city west of here that was one of the great science centers in the ancient days, and more of the Nanes were created there than anywhere else. They were supposed to be programmed for absolute obedience, but as time went on, slow chemical changes in their bodies apparently destroyed their programming. They broke out."

"And your people just let them go?" said Bollard incredulously. "They didn't even try to hunt down those creepy horrors?"

"Efforts to do so were made," said Vreya. "But the Nanes are utterly elusive in the forest. And by then the city was dying, and few people were left; Arkuu was in decay." She added bitterly, "As it has continued to decay, ever since our worlds were closed."

"Which brings us to the main point," said Dilullo. "You and this chap Raul belong to the Open-World party. You two were chosen to contact Ashton's group because you could speak galacto?"

"That is so," said Vreya.

"Did you and Raul tell Ashton you could lead him to this Free-Faring?"

"No!" said Vreya. "We helped him escape, so he could search for it. We only knew the general area where the legends said it was. It was the man McGoun who said he had a way of finding its exact location."

Dilullo looked at Garcia. "How could McGoun find this thing when even the Arkuuns don't know where it is?"

Garcia explained. "McGoun came to Arkuu a year ago, to trade. Actually, he was trying to find out the secret of the Closed Worlds. He pretended his ship was disabled, and hung around. Finally he contacted an Arkuun who had an old record about the Free-Faring. It didn't tell where the thing was, but it told a good bit about its principle. The Free-Faring was described as a force that could detach the electro-encephalographic pattern of the mind from the body, and then send the mind—still conscious and observant—anywhere it wished to go, with incredible speed."

"Oh, for God's sake," snorted Bollard, and reached for the brandy bottle.

Garcia said stubbornly, "I know it sounds wild. But McGoun bought that record secretly for a big price, and then brought it to Randall Ashton. Ashton consulted physicists and psychologists. They said the principle, as described in scientific terms, was sound enough.

"That still doesn't explain how McGoun was going to find the thing," Dilullo pointed out.

Garcia said, "Raul and Vreya had told us the general area where legend put the thing. Ashton intended to find it by a sort of radio-compass. One sensitive to radiation within the wavelengths described by the old Arkuun record."

Dilullo frowned. "A pretty long chance, to bring Ashton all the way here."

"You know what?" said Bollard. "I don't think much of this Ashton. He tolls four people along with him on a harebrained trip to the Closed Worlds, he leaves one of them dying in Yarr while he goes off to chase a legend, and he leaves a crew of eight men here to get slaughtered while he follows his will-of-the-wisp further."

"We're not being paid to like Ashton, but to find him," Dilullo reminded him.

"And how do we do that?" asked Bollard.

"By doing what he did—detecting the radiation of the Free-Faring and going in that direction. You've got a radiation-detector."

Bollard asked Garcia, "What was the wave-length of this radiation?"

Garcia looked guilty. "I don't know. I'm sorry, but that stuff is out of my field. Sattargh set up the instrument. I remember he said this described radiation was a little shorter in wavelength than even gamma rays."

Bollard grunted. "That's a fine precise scientific datum to work on."

"Can't you broaden the sensitivity-band of our detector downward?" demanded Dilullo.

"I can try. But I sure can't do it right now. I'm blown."

Dilullo stood up, stretching wearily. "We all are. This has been a day. Janssen, you relieve Milner for the second watch."

Chane awoke in the middle of the night, where he slept on the floor of the main compartment. It was quite dark, but he could hear breathing and a careful movement.

Then he smiled. They had given Vreya one of the small cabins, but she had come out and was lying down beside him. He couldn't blame her for being scared in there alone.

Next morning, Bollard tinkered for hours with the detector in the control-panel. There was nothing for the others to do but wait. Milner said loudly that this was the devil of a place and he would be glad to get away from it. The others did not bother answering. They sat, with the lasers across their knees, and watched the trees.

Finally Bollard said, "It's hooked up again."

Dilullo went to sit in the pilot's seat beside him, and the others peered over his shoulders. Chane saw the smooth bright lines flowing steadily across the graduated detector-grid.

They waited while Bollard used the sensor-control to rotate the little sensor outside the flier hull, for a full circle around the landscape.

The bright lines remained level and untroubled.

"Nothing," said Bollard.

"If the radiation source is beyond those mountains, we couldn't get it down here. We'll have to go up high."

Bollard nodded. "I was afraid you'd say that. Still, I'd as lief take a chance with Helmer's fliers as with the creepy critters in this forest."

Janssen took the pilot-chair. There was no way they could first scan the sky, for the towering trees all around the clearing barred off the view except directly overhead. They would just have to run their chances.

Janssen taxied the flier out into the clearing. Then he

took them up out of the forest on the VTO drive. With strained eyes and with the questing radar they scanned the sky, but saw no fliers.

They went higher, until they were well above the altitude of even the highest mountains. Then, as they circled, Bollard tried his detector again. It showed no response.

"Ah, I told you this was too vague," he muttered, as he started rotating the sensor. "Probably Ashton himself found that out, and . . ."

He was suddenly silent. Chane, looking over his shoulder, saw that the flowing level lines of light were level no longer. They had flung themselves upward in a sharp loop, quivering wildly, as though they strained toward a mighty heartbeat far away.

"By Heaven. I think we've got it!" said Dilullo.

"We've got something else," said Milner. "We've got company. Lots of company."

And he pointed back through the window, at the fliers coming after them fast.

XII

CHANE LOOKED BACK at the light Arkuun fliers coming after them. There were five of them.

"Helmer's radar may not be as good as ours, but it seems to work," he said.

"Crack on speed, Janssen," said Dilullo. "The direction the sensor was pointing—ten o'clock."

The flier leaped forward. They began to draw away from the pursuers.

Chane looked at Dilullo. "You know, if this is the way to Ashton and the others, that means we're leading Helmer right to them."

"What else are we going to do?" demanded Dilullo. "We can make deceptive maneuvers all over the sky but their radar will find us. Landing and hiding again will get us nowhere. We might as well go on and see if this is the way to Ashton, and worry about the rest later."

Dilullo spoke for the benefit of all of them, and there were no dissenters. Chane laughed, and almost said, *You're beginning to think like a Starwolf!* but he didn't say it.

The mountains came toward them rapidly. High as the flier was, it was not too high above the summits. There was no vegetation at all on the higher slopes, just stone and scree. Under the topaz sun the ranges looked infinitely inhospitable, and the deep valleys between them that were filled with forest were not much more inviting.

The flier bucked and kicked as Janssen fought tremendous drafts. He went higher and things quieted down a bit as they rushed on over the rumpled, tumbled landscape.

The fliers pursuing them were falling behind; the skitter-flier had more speed, though not too much more. That Helmer would follow them as long as he had them on his radar, Chane had not the slightest doubt.

The mountains got worse instead of better as they went on. Chane thought that they made the harsh ranges of Varna look small. Varna was a heavy planet and its gravity held down the effects of diastrophism. But here, long ago, the processes of mountain-building had functioned on a gigantic scale.

What was worse, these ranges did not run in nice parallel lines, but were jumbled helter-skelter, criss-cross, every which way. It looked as though this part of Arkuu had been the playground of colossal children and that they had left the place pretty messed up.

"I can see why something could be hidden up here for a long time," said Chane.

Vreya nodded. "Even the Nanes do not come into these mountains."

The pursuers had dropped back out of sight and they were over what seemed the worst of the mountain-jumble, when Bollard spoke sharply.

"John, take a look at this grid. I don't like it."

Chane could see that the loops on the radiation-detector were now practically throwing themselves off the grid, twitching wildly.

"We don't know what's ahead but whatever it is we're getting bloody close to it—and it's almighty strong."

Dilullo nodded. "Sheer off a bit, Janssen. Thirty degrees."

The flier banked off in a curve. Bollard kept watching the detector. Presently the loops began to diminish in size. He rotated the sensor unit. When it pointed off northwestward instead of north, the loops came on strong again.

"Ah-huh," said Dilullo. "We'll make a wide curve around till we get a closer fix on this thing."

Janssen kept the flier swinging in a wide curve. Bollard kept changing the angle of the detector-sensor. Finally, when they had made a circle of a score of miles across, Bollard pointed.

"Somewhere over in that region," he said, pointing toward a lofty, dark mountain shaped like a flattened cone. "I can't pinpoint it more than that."

"All right, we'll edge over in that direction and see what the scope tells us," Dilullo said.

"I don't think," said Chane, "that we're going to have much time for fancy reconnoitering."

He pointed southward, where five gleaming fliers were coming over the mountains toward them.

Dilullo muttered an oath. But Chane admired the way he then went cold and calculating. Dilullo looked again at the fliers, estimating distance, and then he went to the scope and swung it, peering toward the conical mountain.

Janssen glanced uneasily back at him. "I can't maneuver out of this one, John—not against five fliers."

"Head fast for the base of that mountain," said Dilullo. "The whole area around there is covered with rocks and talus. Helmer's fliers can't land near there but you can put us down with the VTO."

"Your faith in my ability is touching, but it's going to kill us all one of these days," said Janssen. "All right."

He sent the flier into a long oblique rush. The Arkuun fliers were coming up fast now. Apparently the range was too long for their missiles as yet, but Chane felt that they were going to be in range awfully soon.

Janssen slowed their rush and then went into the vertical descent. The conical mountain now loomed up over them like a thundercloud and the drafts around it made the flier kick and shudder as it went down. Below, Chane saw a mass of detritus studded with huge boulders, with only a few possible landing-places. He hoped that Janssen was as good as Dilullo thought he was.

He was that good. He touched them down beside a towering boulder, on a flat area of bare rock no bigger than a house.

"Outside fast, and take the lasers and the emergency packs," said Dilullo. "They'll be over us in a minute!"

They grabbed the weapons and the packs and tumbled out of the flier. There was a screaming in the sky as the Mercs ran like the devil. Dilullo was leading them toward an even bigger boulder a hundred yards away.

"We could have stayed behind the first boulder and had as much cover!" panted Bollard, who hated running.

"I want to draw their fire away from the flier," Dilullo answered shortly. "We're going to need it."

Chane, running easily, took Vreya's arm to help her along. She shook herself loose, angrily.

"I don't need help!"

"No more you do," said Chane, admiring her flashing golden legs.

Then they dived behind the bigger boulder, just as the missiles began going off around them. "Rock-dust and chips of stone blew into their faces, and the explosions seemed deafening.

The fliers screamed by high overhead, heading toward the mountains. But they were already starting to curve around.

"We'll have them back in a moment," said Dilullo. "Shift to the other side of the boulder." He added angrily, "Damn it, Chane—*move!*"

Chane was staring wonderingly at the five fliers. Two of them, the two at one end of their formation, had passed right over the top of the conical mountain.

The other three were coming around and beginning a swoop that would take them lower over the Mercs. But those two were behaving oddly. They drifted away as though out of control, turned their noses downward, and went into a rambling, suicidal dive that crashed them on the rocks not far away.

"What the devil?" began Dilullo, and then cried, "Jump!"

They got around to the other side of the boulder just before the missiles came. This time the boulder took a direct hit on its other side, and heaved up as though about to explode to fragments.

But it settled back, leaving them shaken. They picked themselves up as the fliers screamed on past.

"What brought those two down?" demanded Milner. "We sure didn't."

"I got a good look at the one that crashed nearest to us, just before it hit," said Chane. "The men in it seemed to be dead, their heads hanging, before they even hit the ground."

"They were the only two that went right over the mountain," said Dilullo, staring up at the vast, dark conical mass. He frowned in thought. Then he said, "Chane, you can operate that detector in the flier?"

Chane nodded. "Then get back there fast and get a fix on the radiation again," said Dilullo. "I want to know whether it seems to come from that mountain."

"What's the matter with me going?" demanded Bollard. "I'm the best instrument man here."

"You're also a famous beer-drinker, and fat, and Chane can run twice as fast as you," said Dilullo. "Does that answer your question?"

Chane grinned, and took off. When he was around the boulder and out of sight of the rest of them, he put his Starwolf speed into it, bounding over the broken rock like a panther.

He thought, as he had thought many times before, that Dilullo gave him a lot of the dirty jobs because he knew Chane had that Varnan strength and speed. The devil of it was that he couldn't use it openly without making others suspect his Starwolf origin, and that had got him into some pretty tight pinches.

As he ran he looked away to the east, expecting the Arkuun fliers to come screaming back at them. But the three fliers were circling, not moving back to another attack on the Mercs.

Chane could understand that. Helmer—if Helmer had not been in one of the two crashed fliers—would certainly be cautious now about flying near the mountain.

Chane dived into the flier, and to the cockpit. He turned the detector on, then started rotating the sensor.

When the sensor pointed toward the conical mountain, the detector seemed to go crazy. The strength-indicator loops of light became wild squiggles, as though there wasn't a big enough grid to show what was happening to them.

Chane tried two complete rotations of the sensor and both times it happened. He shut off the instrument, and jumped out of the flier.

Looking eastward, he was surprised to see the three Arkuun fliers going away. When he reached the boulder, the Mercs had come out from behind it. They too were watching the departing fliers.

Chane pretended to pant as he asked, "You think they're scared off?"

"I wish they were," said Dilullo. "But as we were coming down I noticed a flat area miles east of here, big enough for them to land their fliers on. I think they'll be back, on foot. We've not got all the time in the world."

Chane told him of what the detector had revealed. Dilullo's horse-like face got longer as he looked up at the huge bulk of the conical mountain.

"Then whatever makes the radiation is on the mountain," he said. "Has to be. If the source was further away, the mountain itself would block the detector."

"Then that's where Ashton went?" said Bollard. "Where this Free-Faring is supposed to be?"

"We'll hope so."

Bollard shook his head. "It gets crazier. A multi-millionaire nutty enough to come to a hole like this chasing a myth about the Free-Faring. And then those Arkuuns in the two fliers tumbling dead out of the sky, just like that."

"Maybe they weren't dead," said Vreya.

Chane looked at her. "I saw them, Vreya. I saw them as they fell.

"Maybe their minds had been released from their bodies," she said. "That's what the Free-Faring was supposed to do. Maybe that's why they fell."

XIII

From high up in the windy darkness, on a ledge a third of the way up the mountain, Chane stared down with Dilullo and Bollard.

"Nothing yet," he said. "Maybe they won't try it till daylight."

"They'll try it," said Dilullo. "I've seen a lot of men, and these Arkuuns are some of the toughest. Besides, there'll be one of the moons up in a few minutes."

They continued to watch and listen, looking down the narrow, twisting path by which they had ascended. Presently there was an elfin shimmer of light from the horizon and the nearer of the two silver-pink moons floated up into the sky.

They had got up here just as night was falling. There had been a short, frenzied time of activity down below, before they left. As Allubane set, they had worked feverishly to get out of the flier all their gear that they might need.

Milner and Janssen had come back from scouting, just as it was getting dark. Milner had found what they were looking for, a nest of tall rocks not too far away, in which the flier could be hidden with the hope that it would not be too easily found.

In the twilight, Janssen had done a marvellous job of piloting, taking the flier up only a few yards and hedge-hopping with it and putting it down amid the concealing rocks of that nest. Then he had come running back and they had shouldered their packs and started for the mountain.

They found the path almost at once. It looked as though it had been worn by the feet of ages, twisting here and there amid the beetling rocks and crags, going steadily up the steep slope. They reached this ledge just as complete darkness fell, and here they stopped. The others were chewing rations farther along the ledge, while Chane and Bollard and Dilullo, their lasers in their hands, had gone down and watched the path.

"You hear anything?" Bollard asked Chane. "I notice you've got keen ears."

"Not a thing," said Chane.

The second moon came up, perpetually chasing the first one, and the tarnished silver light became stronger.

Chane saw Dilullo peering intently downward, his harsh face made harsher by the light.

"They're down there," said Dilullo. "And they'll try it sooner or later. I wish I had a guarantee we'll live the night out."

Chane grinned. "What do you care? You've got no wife and children to worry about."

Dilullo said in a flat voice, "That's right, I haven't. All right, I'll watch from a little higher up. I'll have Milner and Janssen relieve you in three hours."

Dilullo turned and went back up the path. Bollard looked after him, watching him go in the silver light.

When Dilullo was out of sight, Bollard did a thing that utterly amazed Chane. He turned and struck Chane with all his force, with a flat hand across the face.

Bollard was flat and sloppy but he was strong. Chane staggered back against an outcropping boulder beside the path. Bollard came in and grabbed him by the collar.

It was not the moon-faced, cheery Bollard now. Bollard had been a Merc for many years and you did not live years like that without some iron in you, and all the iron showed in his moonlit face as he glared at Chane.

"You ever say a thing like that again and I'll kill you, Chane," he said, his fist raised.

Chane was too astonished even to lift his hands. "What ..." he began.

Bollard lowered his fist. "You mean you don't know? John never told you?"

"Told me what?" demanded Chane.

"You made that crack about John having no wife and children," said Bollard. "He had them once, years ago. A beautiful wife and a little boy and a girl. He came back with me from a mission to Spica, to find there'd been a fire in his house and all three of them dead."

Bollard looked down the moonlit, rocky slope. "I remember that after the funeral, I went with John where his house had been, and we looked at the ashes. He kept saying to me, 'It doesn't make sense, that a man can fly to the stars and yet lose his whole family in a stinking, lousy fire. It just doesn't make sense.'"

Chane was silent. Then he said, "I'll be back in a moment," and went up the path.

Dilullo was standing where the path joined the ledge, looking and listening, his laser gleaming in the moonlight.

"John," said Chane. "I didn't know. I'm sorry . . ."

"For Godalmighty's sake," said Dilullo. "Now I've heard everything. A Starwolf making an apology. In the whole galaxy, nobody would believe it."

Then he changed his tone and growled, "Get back down there where you're supposed to be, Chane. And forget it. You couldn't know."

Chane said nothing, but turned and went back down the path.

They had watched for more than two hours when they heard sounds. Sounds of feet on rock and grit, trying to be quiet but still audible.

"They're coming," muttered Bollard. "But we won't be

able to see them to use the lasers till they're right on us. This is going to be murder. Literally."

"You watch," said Chane. "Maybe I can discourage them a little."

He put down his laser and went to the boulder beside the path and leaned against it. It held firm. He put into his arms and legs all the strength that Varna had given him, and pushed.

The boulder heaved, a very little. He pushed further, and then all of a sudden the boulder came out of the soil and toppled and rolled. It went down the moonlit slope with a mighty noise, clashing against other rocks, bounding and bumping and raising the devil altogether.

They heard a muffled exclamation from down the slope, and a sound of feet moving fast, and then nothing but the receding bump and clash of the big rock going faster and faster down to the valley.

Chane picked up his laser. "I don't think it got any of them—it rolled wide of the path. But it may make them decide to wait till daylight."

Bollard stared open-mouthed. "How in the world could you push a rock that size?"

"It was just barely balanced on the slope," Chane lied. "I felt it sway a little when you banged me back against it."

Dilullo came down and listened with them. There were no more stealthy sounds from below.

"They'll wait for daylight," Dilullo said. "Which means we'd better be on our way well before the sun rises."

Janssen came down presently to relieve Chane.

"What's that lump inside your coverall?" demanded Dilullo.

Unwillingly, Janssen fished out the half-full bottle of brandy. "Thought I'd bring this along, for emergencies."

"Good thinking, Janssen," said Dilullo. "For that, you can have a drink of it."

Janssen's face brightened in the moonlight.

"When you've finished your watch," said Dilullo, and took the bottle from his hand and went up the path.

Chane followed him up to the ledge. Milner was sleeping. Garcia was not in sight. Vreya was sitting and looking up at the sky in which the two moons now rode royally amid the glittering stars of the Perseus Arm. Chane went over and sat down beside her.

"So many stars," she said, in a low voice, and then added passionately, "and we cannot go to them, we must stay forever on our little worlds."

She lowered her gaze and looked at Chane. "You have been to many of them?"

"Not in this Arm," Chane said. "But to many stars . . . yes."

She gripped his hand. "I believe now that the Free-Faring is here, Chane. Very near to us. The gateway to the stars."

He stared at her incredulously. "You can't really think that a man's mind could leave his body and go starfaring?"

"I do think it," she said. Her clear-cut face was rapt. "What I have always dreamed of—the freedom of the universe. And perhaps close . . . very close."

She looked up again at the glistening vault above. Of a sudden, Chane got a strange, chilling feeling that not only did she believe it, but that it might be true.

There was a sound of running feet, and Chane grabbed his laser and sprang up. But it was Garcia who came running from farther along the ledge.

"I've found something," he said. "Not a hundred yards farther along here. Some kind of a passage . . ."

Dilullo got up and he and Chane followed Garcia. They came to a place where there was a cliff of rock right above the ledge. There was enough moonlight to show them the dark opening of a tunnel leading into the rock.

"No hand-lamps till we get well inside," said Dilullo. They went in, moving cautiously, for the darkness in the tunnel was intense. The floor under their feet seemed perfectly level and smooth. When they had gone a score of steps, Dilullo flashed on his hand-lamp.

Chane looked around wonderingly. They stood in a big man-made tunnel of softly gleaming metal. It was like a square with an arch on top, in cross-section, and it was at least twenty feet across.

It ran straight into the heart of the mountain as far as they could see.

"Some kind of old aqueduct?" said Garcia puzzledly.

"No," said Dilullo. "I think this is a road to something."

Yes, thought Chane. *A road to something. To the Free-Faring?*

He shook off the thought. Vreya's talk was starting to make him think old impossible myths could be true.

"Maybe it's just a blind alley?"

Chane shook his head. "You can feel a strong draft of air coming through from ahead. It opens out somewhere."

Dilullo made his decision. "We're going in. It may be the way Ashton went. At the worst, this tunnel could be far more easily defended than that ledge on the mountainside. Chane, get all the others and bring them here. With all our gear."

When Chane had brought them, Dilullo gave them no time to stare around. He started down the straight tunnel, with Bollard beside him and both their hand-lamps beamed ahead.

There was nothing at all to see. Their boots made echoes in the big metal tube and the echoes were now ahead of them and now behind them, so that the ears were confused. Chane stopped twice and beamed his lamp behind them, under the impression of following footsteps.

The thing went on and on. They were going, straight as an arrow, deep into the heart of the mountain. And still that cool breeze from ahead hit their faces.

The breeze got stronger. The echoes from ahead sounded different.

"Hold it," said Dilullo.

Ahead, the tunnel seemed to debouch into a vast, vaguely lit space.

"Now we'll take this easy," said Dilullo. "Remember what happened to the men in those two fliers. I'll have a look."

Dilullo went forward slowly, until he seemed to stand on the very brink. They saw his head turn this way and that, gazing.

He stood there for what seemed to Chane a long time before he turned around and motioned them forward. They went, with slow steps.

Chane's first impression when he stood at the end of the tunnel was that it opened into the side, not the bottom, of a vast well.

There was no doubt at all that this colossal shaft was man-made, for it was lined with the same gleaming metal as the tunnel. It was at least a thousand feet in diameter, and high above them it was open to the sky. Oblique moonlight struck down and was reflected from the gleaming walls.

There was a wide ledge all around the well, level with the tunnel in whose mouth they stood. They stepped out onto the ledge and peered down. Far, far below them lay the floor of the gigantic shaft. They could see it because it had light down there from another source than the moonlight above.

The light came from an area a hundred feet in diameter, exactly centered in the floor of the gigantic shaft. This area was not smooth but consisted of countless facets, and the facets glowed with a cold blue light, not at all intense but with a strange quality in it that Chane had never seen before.

"Look there!" said Bollard, pointing.

Chane saw now what he had missed in the first stunning impression of the place.

At four points equally spaced around the ledge, wide walks of massive metal ran out into the well. They ran to a circular platform of what looked like glass, exactly the same size as the blue-glowing area on the floor below, and situated exactly above the latter.

Three men lay unmoving on the glass plate out there. One wore the costume of Arkuu, and the other two were dressed in coveralls.

Dilullo twisted the focus of his lamp and sent a long narrow beam at one of the latter two, who lay face upward.

"Ashton!" cried Garcia. "And he's dead!"

From far around the well, from the shadowy ledge hundreds of feet away, a voice spoke dully.

"Not dead," it said. "Not dead, but gone. Gone on the Free-Faring."

XIV

"McGoun!" exclaimed Garcia, and a figure advanced out of the shadows.

"Garcia," it said. "And who are these?"

Garcia babbled explanations. As he did so, Dilullo sized up Jewett McGoun.

A stocky middle-aged man who at the moment looked older than he was. His flat, seamy face quivered with self-pity, and his dark eyes were rimmed with red and seemed about to burst into tears at any moment.

"You don't know what I've been through, Garcia," he said. "None of you . . ."

Dilullo's voice cracked like a whip. "Chane! You and Milner watch that tunnel."

Chane nodded and went with Milner to the place where the tunnel debouched onto the ledge. But from there he could see and hear McGoun.

McGoun was practically crying. "A billion dollars. Maybe many billions. Right here, for the taking away. And Ashton . . ."

"What about Ashton?" asked Garcia. "You said he had gone on the Free-Faring? And what about Sattargh?"

McGoun pointed to the glass platform suspended out there over the pit.

"There they are. And Raul, too. They had to try the Free-Faring. They wouldn't be content just to find its secret and then sell it. Billions! But they had to try it . . ."

Dilullo's voice did the whip-crack again. "Let's not have so much weeping. Exactly what happened?"

McGoun knuckled his moist eyes. "Don't push me around. I've been pushed around too much. All alone here, for weeks and weeks. They would come back to their bodies and I'd plead with them, and they wouldn't even listen to me. They'd just eat, and drink, and stare at me, and then go back out there."

"Come back to their bodies?" cried Bollard. "What are you trying to give us?"

McGoun looked dully at him. "You don't believe it? You walk out onto that grid and see. I tried it—it was terrifying. I came right back to my body and I wouldn't try it again. But Ashton and the others kept going and going . . ."

"Oh, nuts," said Bollard. He told Dilullo, "John, if that's Ashton's body out there, we'll need it, to take back to Earth for identification. I'll go out and get it."

"Now wait," said Dilullo. "Let's wait a minute before we do anything foolish."

"Let him go," said McGoun, his face sodden with resentment. "He's so damned ready to call me a liar. Let him try it."

"Where's the flier you came in?" Dilullo asked.

McGoun made a gesture. "Down below that side of the mountain. But it's no good without Ashton. You know—when I threatened to take the flier and go if they didn't quit the Free-Faring, Ashton took and hid some of the small parts. Without them the flier can't operate."

Chane, sitting with his laser across his knees just clear of the tunnel-mouth, glanced toward Vreya. She had not spoken. But she stood there, her eyes brilliant with emotion, gazing toward the glassy disk out there on which the three men lay.

She looked, he thought, like someone who after long hope and despair sees the gateway of a prison stand open and inviting. He began to wonder. Could what McGoun said be true? Could the men out there be, not dead, but with their minds set free to range all the universe at will?

The hackles came up on Chane's neck at the thought. He did not like such an idea at all. He had been a Starwolf and a free ranger and raider, but physically. Everything in his Varnan training made him recoil from a concept such as this one of using your mind to rove without your body.

A sudden thought came to Chane. Was this Free-Faring what the Varnans had found when they came to raid the Closed Worlds, long ago? Had the thing seemed as repulsive to them as it did to him, a thing from which they would recoil? Was that why Starwolves had been forbidden ever to go to Allubane?

"I tell you, it's true," McGoun was saying, in a high, sobbing voice. "Look, you don't have to take my word. Just walk out there on the grid and see what happens to you."

Chane noticed that Bollard still looked skeptical, but that Dilullo had a look on his face as though he was not too sure.

"You tell me that this thing can take a man's mind and release it from his body . . ." he began.

"It *can!*" cried McGoun. He pointed down to the floor of the giant shaft, where the central circle glowed with cold blue light. "That down there. It emits a force, straight upward. A column of quite invisible force. The glass-looking grid out there is transparent to it."

And if that is so, Chane thought, the force would strike right on up into the sky, and would hit the two Arkuun fliers and cause the thing that had happened to them.

"You tell them, Garcia," appealed McGoun. "I'm not a scientist; I'm a trader, trying to make an honest profit. I wish to God now I'd never heard of this thing."

Garcia said, hesitatingly, "All I know of the theory of it is what Ashton told me. The glowing area down there is matter so treated as to emit a subtle force perpetually. The force is one that *amplifies* the power of that electric pattern in the brain which we call the mind. It gives the mind-pattern such great power that it can break loose from the synaptic structure in the brain. It can go where it wills, short-cutting the three dimensions by driving across dimensions of which we know nothing. It can return, and affix itself to the brain again, and reactivate the body."

"Oh, for God's sake . . ." Bollard began.

Chane whirled and triggered his laser back into the long tunnel. The flash and crack were tremendous in that closed space.

They ran to the tunnel, keeping clear of its mouth. Dilullo looked enquiringly at Chane.

Chane shook his head. "Nobody coming. Just a stone or something someone threw into the tunnel, to see if anybody was on guard. I thought I'd better let them know we're here."

"This is a nice spot," Dilullo muttered. He turned and asked McGoun, "Is there another way out of here?"

McGoun shook his head. "No way but the tunnel."

"Then they've got us nicely boxed," said Dilullo. "We've got rations and some water in our packs, but we can't hold out here forever."

"Look," said Bollard. "There's no need to hold out forever. We'll get Ashton's body off that grid—if it's dangerous to go near it, we can snake it off with a rope. We'll come out of the tunnel with all lasers going and cut right through them."

"Ashton will die if you do that," warned McGoun. "His mind can't regain his body unless it's out there on the grid, in the force of the Free-Faring."

Bollard looked as though he was about to make a highly profane reply, but Dilullo held up a hand and silenced him.

"What's that?"

A voice came booming down the tunnel, a man's strong voice speaking as through a long tube.

"I am Helmer. Can I come in truce?"

Dilullo said admiringly, "That man's got guts. He must know that one laser blast down the tunnel would cut him down."

"Well, do we cut him down?" asked Milner hopefully.

"No, we don't," said Dilullo. "Bollard, you've got the loudest mouth here when you want to use it. Call to him that he can come in truce."

Bollard obeyed. They waited. Then they began to hear a man's steps echoing down to them through the long metal tube. They were firm steps, strongly planted, and they got louder and louder, and then Helmer stepped out of the tunnel and stood looking at them.

In the vague light, Helmer seemed twice as impressive as he had in sunlight, his blond head erect, his mighty arms and legs all sculptured muscle, his bleak, icy eyes surveying them one by one.

Then Helmer turned his gaze out into the vastness of the shaft. He looked at the grid and the three motionless bodies on it, and then down at the glowing circle below.

A kind of agony came upon his face as he looked. He seemed to speak rather to himself, than to them.

"So it is true, and there is one of the evil things still left. And after all this time, it has been found."

His lips compressed. He seemed to stand and think for a moment, before he turned and spoke to them.

"Listen to me, strangers. This thing you have searched for and found has great and luring powers. That is true. But also it is a greatly evil thing."

"What evil would come from a thing that is supposed merely to free the mind from the body?" asked Dilullo.

Helmer's eyes flashed cold flame. "You saw the dead cities in the jungle? Go ask them! They were great and living cities once. But each of them had a thing like this, the instrument of the Free-Faring. And the sterile life of the mind was more alluring than the real life of the body, and hundreds by hundreds, century after century, the people of those cities went into the Free-Faring and clung to it until they died."

He looked around their faces again. "The people of the cities withered away, the life dwindled. Until finally a group arose, determined to destroy the Free-Faring and save our people from its insidious corruption. In one city after another, the gateways—like this one—were destroyed. But those who were addicted to the Free-Faring tried to save it, and we have always known that at least one of the gateways remained hidden and intact. Because of that, we determined to close our worlds to strangers, so that not all the galaxy would flock here searching for it. As you have searched—and found."

Dilullo shook his head. "The thing is only an instrument of science. If it does what they tell me it can do, it could be a very noble instrument for all men."

Helmer flung out his hand and pointed toward the three unmoving bodies out on the central grid.

"Look at those who have tasted the Free-Faring! Do they look ennobled? Or do they look drunken, sodden—like dying men?"

"I agree," said Chane.

Helmer turned and looked at him. "Stranger, when I saw you before, I thought that you were more of a man than any outworlder I had met. Now I see that you think like a man."

"I do *not* agree!" cried Vreya. Her face was passionate as she looked stormily at Helmer. "It was fanatics like you who took away from us the freedom of the stars." She turned and pointed at the glass grid, where the three men lay unmoving. "That is the road to infinite freedom, to go anywhere in the universe, to find out anything we wish to know—and you would destroy it."

"I *will* destroy it," said Helmer. "It almost destroyed us, long ago. I will not have this hateful vice corrupt our people again—or any other people."

He turned to Dilullo. "This is what you can do. You can gather your people and go, and we will strike no blow at you."

"But," said Dilullo, "they tell me that if Ashton and the other two are taken off that grid, their minds cannot rejoin their bodies."

"That is the truth," said Helmer. "And it is well. They will be living logs until they die, and that is their punishment."

"No," said Dilullo decisively. "It is the safety of Ashton that is our job, and we cannot do that to him."

"Then," said Helmer slowly, "you will all perish when we destroy the Free-Faring. The choice is yours."

He turned his back on them and strode toward the tunnel. Milner, his teeth showing in a soundless snarl, started to raise his laser but Dilullo knocked it down. Helmer went on into the tunnel.

Chane saw Dilullo turn and give him a cold stare. "Why did you say you agree with him?"

Chane shrugged. "Because I do. I think a thing like this is better destroyed."

"You're a fool and a coward," Vreya said to him. "You're afraid of something you can't understand, afraid of the Free-Faring."

"Frankly, I am," said Chane. He pointed with his laser to the unmoving men out on the grid. "If that's what this fine achievement does to a man, I want no part of it."

He looked back to Dilullo. "Now what?"

"That," said Dilullo, "is the kind of a question that makes a Merc leader wish he wasn't a leader."

"Accept Helmer's terms!" McGoun broke in. His soiled cheeks quivered. "Ashton didn't care about me, all alone here. Why risk getting killed for him?"

"Because," said Dilullo between his teeth, "we signed a

111

contract, and Mercs who break one are thrown out of the guild. It was you, McGoun, with your nosing around in other world's secrets and your hankering for money, who brought us all here. Now shut up."

"But what *do* we do?" asked Bollard.

"We wait," said Dilullo. "We wait till Ashton and the other two come back to their bodies—if what McGoun has said is true—and we grab them, and then we fight our way out."

The great shaft was darkening as the moons of Arkuu slid further down the sky, so that little of their light now penetrated.

Dilullo told Janssen and Bollard to take the second watch at the tunnel, and that they had all better get some sleep. They curled up silently, along the back of the ledge, and presently were asleep. All but Vreya.

Chane watched her. She was sitting and staring almost fixedly at the grid out there, and the three motionless figures on it. She watched it for a long time, before she too stretched out to sleep.

Milner looked around the vast, darkening place. "That ruined city was bad enough," he muttered. "This is worse."

"Don't talk," said Chane. "If any of them try coming through the tunnel, our hearing will be our best warning."

But, looking around, he had to agree that Milner was right. He had never been in a place so curiously oppressive. It was not so much the place itself as the knowledge of what is could to do a man, drive the mind out of his body, make him like one dead. The strong repulsion to that idea stirred in Chane again.

The hours seemed long before their watch ended. Janssen and Bollard, when roused, grunted and took their places at the tunnel, Bollard yawning prodigiously.

Chane took his boots off and stretched out, but he found that sleep came slowly. He still felt the oppression. It seemed to stifle him. He kept thinking of the three shadowy forms out on that dim grid, wondering where their minds were and what they were doing; wondering what it was like to be a disembodied mind; wondering if they would ever come back. After a time he did sleep, and he had something almost unheard of for him: nightmares.

He woke out of one with a start. There had been a sound, not the occasional stirrings of Bollard and Janssen as they sat staring down the tunnel, but a new, small sound.

He looked around sharply. Vreya was gone.

Chane got to his feet. His gaze swept the vast, darkened space. Then he saw her.

She was walking silently out onto one of the metal walks that led to the central grid. The two guards, their backs to her, had not seen her.

She was going to the Free-Faring . . .

Chane moved with the swiftness and silence of a hunting cat. His unshod feet made no sound. He went in great noiseless bounds after the tall golden girl who walked out toward the grid, over the abyss, as though she went to a lover.

He would reach her in time to pull her back, if she did not turn . . .

At that moment, warned by instinct or the sound of his breathing, Vreya turned.

She flashed him a fierce, wild look and then started to run forward.

Four great strides and a spring and he could catch her before she stepped onto the grid. Chane strode and sprang, and he did catch her right at the edge.

But he had forgotten how strong Vreya was. Even as he caught hold of her, she threw herself forward onto the smooth grid. Chane, holding her, was dragged by her wild surge onto the grid with her.

Next instant, Chane felt his brain explode, and he fell into eternity.

XV

It was not quite a fall. Rather it was as though a great hand, gently but very strong, had grasped, lifted, and flung him outward, and he scudded, stunned and helpless, across a silent nothingness.

He was nothing, alone in nothingness.

He was dead, a soul, a spirit, a palmful of electric impulses tossed out naked among the stars. Now he knew what it was like to be that way.

He was afraid.

And he was angry. Raging, that this violation should have been done to him.

He screamed, a fierce eagle scream that defied the whole cosmos. He could not hear the scream, but he could sense it as a red flash in the nothingness. And it was answered.

"Don't be afraid, Chane. Don't be angry. Look. Look around you . . ."

Vreya. Of course, Vreya. He was not alone. Vreya . . .

"Look, Chane Look at the stars. Look at the universe." She was not talking. There was no voice in that tremendous silence. Yet he sensed her meaning as he had sensed his own outcry. Her words crashed against his consciousness like a sunburst, all golden and glorious. *"We're free, Chane! Free!"*

He tried to orient himself toward her, tried to see her, and in doing that he saw instead the universe.

The black, black beautiful deeps that ran to the rim of creation, the dark All-Mother with a billion galaxies spangling her breast and the stars like fireflies at her fingertips, and he could see it all, clear and clean. The stars burned with a pure radiance. The coiling nebula glowed, silver clouds against the primal black. All down the long, long darkness the scattered galaxies wheeled and flashed, and he could hear them, and he realized that the nothingness was not silent. It moved and sang with the movements of the suns, the worlds, the moons, the comets, the gaseous clouds, the banks of drift, the cosmic dust and the free atoms, the star-swarms and the galaxies. Nothing was still, and he understood that this was because stillness was death, and therefore forbidden. The universe lived, moved, beat with a vital pulse. . . .

And he was part of it. He too throbbed and moved, caught up in the great cosmic dancing, the Brownian Movement of the universe. Movement of the universe. This evoked a memory, of his body floating in a great sea, becoming one with the life, the pulse, the movement of the sea.

"Vreya!" He called to her, without thinking how he did it. *"Vreya, come back with me!"* The panic that went with the impulse was black, an ugly black that blotted out the radiance. The memory of his body had done that, reminding him that he was not an atom but a man with a face and a name, Morgan Chane, the Starwolf. He looked somehow down, although there was neither up nor down, and saw his body sprawled on the grid beside Ashton and Sattargh and Raul. It was sprawled together with Vreya's body, and they looked like the newly dead, mouths slack, eyes glazed, arms and legs flung wide in limp abandonment. He yearned toward his body.

"Vreya, come!"

She was close beside him now. He could sense her there, a tiny patch of sparkling motes.

"You are afraid," she said, contemptuously. *"Go back, then. Get your feet on the nice safe ground."*

"Vreya . . . !"

"A lifetime . . . waited . . . dreaming . . . now I have it, I am free, free of the stars, free of the universe. Good bye, Chane."

"Vreya!" He flung himself toward the sparkling motes, and he felt her laugh.

"No, you can't hold me now. Do what you will, you can't hold me."

She danced away. The Perseus Arm swung like a burning scythe through the dark behind her, a million stars piled high and shouting as they swung; their voices struck Chane's being and made each separate impulse flare with their splendor. Vreya's tiny gleaming brightened. Once more he felt her laughter, and then she was gone, lost in the blaze of the Perseus suns.

Chane hesitated. He could go back now, revive that disgustingly lax shell that awaited him, make it a man again. Or he could go after Vreya, try again to bring her back . . .

If he let her go she might never come back. She was drunken with the Free-Faring, enough to forget the needs of her body until it was too late, until the beautiful shell perished from lack of food and water. And that would be a waste, a terrible waste. He would never forgive himself if that happened . . .

Really? asked one little mote of him, of the rest of him. *Has the Starwolf truly become noble . . . or is he lying to himself? Does he want secretly to taste a little more of this Free-Faring that so revolts him?*

Chane hung shivering while the toppling blaze of the Perseus Arm swept toward him . . . or was he sweeping toward it? How did you move in this Free-Faring, how did you direct yourself?

Vreya's laughter came to him, faint and distant. *"This way, Chane. It's easy, if you would only stop fighting it. Can't you feel the currents? Like great winds . . . This way . . . This way. . . ."*

He felt the currents They ran between the suns, between the galaxies, lacing the whole together. You caught one and rode it, in the wild twinkling of a second, across distances that would take even a swift Starwolf ship months to span. You fetched up, dazed and shaken, to dance in the whipping corona of a green star, and then go sliding down the little currents that held the green star's worlds around it, calling for Vreya, looking for her, finding her and chasing her through an atmosphere that was the color of a smoky emerald, above strange seas and stranger continents, and there was life there, and her voice made running streaks of silver across his consciousness, crying, "*Oh . . . oh . . . oh!*" in wonder.

And you went on again, pleading with her. You shot a nebula, wrapped in cold fire, and you peered at the drowned suns and the worlds that never saw any other star but their own and no sky but the perpetual icy burning of the cloud. Some of the worlds were barren and some were not, and once Vreya made such a darkness of fear against his mind that he thought she would listen to him and return. But she only darted away, riding the currents like a fleeting spark, toward a cluster of orange suns all mellow as grandfathers, with pretty little planets around their knees. After a while your forgot to plead. You did not really care any more whether Vreya came back to her beautiful body or left it to rot in the crater on Arkuu. You did not even care whether you went back to your own body or not. Because you realized that Vreya was right, and you were wrong.

You realized that the Free-Faring was worth everything. What was the death of a body, a mortal body that would die anyway? What was the death of a city, or a culture, or even a planet—though the planet wouldn't really die, of course, just because men were gone from it. What even was the joy of being a Starwolf, compared to this?

For a Starwolf was planet-bound and ship-bound. Everywhere he went he must take with him air and water and food and atmospheric pressure, or he would perish just like the lesser breeds. He could only go so fast, and so far. Compared to this Free-Faring, it seemed to Chane that he and his fellows had been no more than weak and clumsy children on those Starwolf raids. Now he was free of all those limitations, the frail and dragging flesh and the heavy shell of iron in which it must huddle, ignominiously. Free, Vreya had said, of the stars and the whole universe, and it was true. He could possess it all, comprehend it all. He could go anywhere he wanted to, fleet, disembodied, safe, timeless.

Anywhere.

Even to Varna.

And he went, forgetting Vreya.

He rode the currents swift as a dream, and the remembered sun blazed before him, tawny gold. He had seen it countless times before but always through a screening viewport or from the planet itself; never like this, undimmed, naked and true. He watched the great storms sweep across it, flaming whirlwinds as big as continents. He watched the bright corona, the whipped banners and the darting, arcing falls of fire. The voice of the sun spoke to him, and even though he knew now that the stars spoke to the whole universe and not to tiny bits of it, he took it for a welcome.

Varna came rolling from behind the sun, a blue and copper ball. He sped to meet it, and on the way he met a Starwolf squadron coming in.

How many times, he thought. *How many times!*

He went in with them, pacing them down, though he could have left them far behind. There were five ships. They must have run into trouble, because two of them showed fresh scars. But he knew how it would be inside the ships, and he was pleased, remembering.

They went with a rush, the five ships and the little patch of glowing motes, down through the atmosphere, screaming, ripping the clouds asunder, sending a long roll of thunder crashing down the sky. And then the city was be-low them, Krak, the chief city of the Starwolves, a vast loose-jointed sprawl of stone buildings scattered broadcast over a craggy countryside. Each wolf must have his own den, each Varnan his castle, with breathing room around it and a stout wall against predators, in case of a falling-out.

The starport was east of the city, where the rough land fell away to a great plain, burned golden-brown with sum-mer. Chane hung aside and watched the ships go in for a landing, and there was a sadness in his attenuated being. This was home.

The flags broke out from the buildings of the city, bright spots of color against the dull red stone. Traffic began to move down along the road to the starport; ground-cars, people on foot, long vans for the loot.

The ships' ports opened, and Chane slipped lower, weight-less, soundless, riding the air.

The Starwolves came out of the ships.

My people. My brothers. My fighting mates. I know them. Berkt ... Ssarn ... Vengant ... Chroll ...

My brothers.

But they drove me out!

He watched them, the tall powerful men who walked like tigers, muscles gliding under the fine gold-furred skin. He saw the bright-skinned women come from the city, strong women fit for men like these; they laughed and hung the men with garlands of late flowers and brought them the Varnan wine to drink. Chane remembered the pungent dusty sweetness of the garlands and the lovely violence of the wine. No Earthman could drink that wine and stand. None but he, who was Varnan born.

But they drove me out!

He flitted over them, proud and contemptuous. *I am here. You cannot keep me out, you cannot hold me, you cannot kill. For I am greater now than all of you. I see the weak-ness of your iron bodies, the dullness of your iron ships. I am a Free-Farer, and already I have done things that your feebleness could not endure.*

It was too bad that they could not see him, could not hear his words. They went on drinking and laughing and kissing the women, tossing their heads and squinting their bright cat eyes against the sun. Men and boys from the city brought the loot from the ships and piled it on the long vans. The raiders climbed onto big open ground-cars and rode with their women back into the city, singing as they went.

You have seen them, Chane thought. *Their weakness and their worthlessness. It is time to go now, back to the stars.*

But he did not go, and he wondered if it was possible for a Free-Farer to weep. And that was a strange thought, for he had not once thought of weeping since he was a tiny child in that house, there by the market-place, the one with the snarling masks carved on the rainspouts. Starwolves did not cry.

He moved closer to the house. The little church beside it had long ago fallen into ruin. He hovered outside a tall window, remembering how his mother had tried to furnish the great barren room exactly like the parlor in Carnarvon, and how dwarfed and pallid the furniture had looked compared to the untidy splendors he saw in the rooms of his Varnan playmates. The Reverend Thomas would not have one scrap of the sinful loot beneath his roof.

There was plenty of it there now. A Varnan family had lived there many years, since the outworlders died. Chane himself had lived in the bachelor's quarters, a long sprawling sort of barracks on the other side of the market-place, since he was old enough to go out with the raiding ships.

And they drove me out. Because I killed, in a fair fight, one of them—and they could remember only that I was not of their blood.

He felt not like a Free-Farer but like a ghost.

Time to go . . .

It was night, and the great market-square was a blaze of light. Varnans from the ships and from all parts of the city thronged it, making the stone walls ring. They looked at the heaped loot in the center of the square, and they talked to the raiders and gave them wine and listened to the story of the raid. Berkt had been the leader this time, and he was a great story-teller. Chane listened, rocking on the night wind. How they had struck three different systems, and fought, and come away. Berkt's deep voice rang as he talked. His eyes were yellow and bright, and the other raiders shouted with him, and drank, and held their women. The loot sparkled. Chane rocked like thistledown on the wind, a misty nothing lost in the blaze of light, ignored in the hot vitality of life.

Physical life. They had *done.* They had *felt;* the hammering of the blood, the exquisite visceral pain of mingled fear and excitement, the shock of battle, the joy of physical mastery over body and mind and ship when those elements became a single organism dedicated to survival. Now they were here, breathing the night wind, enjoying their triumph. They could drink, and hold their golden women in their arms; they could laugh and sing, the Varnan songs that made him remember another place and another song, far away. . . . Even in Carnarvon, those men were better off than he. They were not Starwolves, but they too could drink and laugh and fight, and take another man's hand in friendship.

And he . . . he was nothing. A wisp, a sterility, to wander forever looking at wonders he could neither touch nor experience; a useless ghost gathering futile knowledge with which he could accomplish nothing.

He remembered Helmer. He remembered his own body, not as beautiful as these gold-furred brothers of his, but a good strong able active body, tossed away like a discarded glove on an ash heap. He remembered Vreya. And he was sick, in every fleck of this that was now his being.

Sick, and in a panic. What might have happened to his body, while he was busy playing among the stars?

Now indeed it was time to go.

He went, with the roaring voices of the Starwolves echoing in his memory, drowning out the vast impersonal singing of the stars.

Riding the currents, driven by fear, whipped by a wild necessity to be clothed again in flesh, he rushed toward the Perseus Arm. And as he rushed, he called.

"Vreya! Vreya!"

For what seemed an eternity she did not answer, and then he heard her, far away and petulant.

"What is it, Chane? I thought you'd left me."

"Vreya, listen. You must come back . . ."

"No. Too much to see . . . No end, Chane, never an end, isn't it wonderful? Never . . ."

Now he knew what he had to say.

"But there will be an end, Vreya. Very soon."

"How? What?"

"Helmer. He will destroy the Free-Faring if we don't go back and stop him. It will be gone forever, and we with it. Hurry, Vreya!"

She said crossly, *"What about your friends?"*

"There aren't enough of them. They need us, all of us . . . Raul, and Sattargh, and Ashton too. Call them, Vreya. Search for them. Tell them to come back, tell them to hurry, before Helmer destroys them."

Some of his panic had communicated itself to her. He could feel it. *"Yes, he would do that. He said he would. Destroy the Free-Faring, destroy our bodies . . . and we would die. He mustn't do that. . . ."*

"Then hurry!"

"Where are you going, Chane?"

"Back," he said. *"Back to help them fight."*

And he fled, a bodiless terror, back across the singing stars to Arkuu and a hollow mountain, where a man named Morgan Chane lay dead, or sleeping. . . .

XVI

CHANE WOKE TO A sound of thunder. It echoed away and then came again. It did not sound exactly like thunder, though. He tried to open his eyes to see what it was.

His eyes?

Yes. He had eyes, human eyes that flinched from the glare of the sun. He had human flesh again, and bones that ached from being too long in one position, sprawled heavily on the unyielding grid.

He was back.

He lay still for a moment, listening to his own breathing, the sound of the blood moving in his veins. Just to be sure, he clenched his hands, gripping his humanness, so thankful that he could feel it as a kind of joyous pain. Then he got his eyelids open and stared dazedly upward.

He saw the circle of yellow daylight at the top of the shaft, the sun-blaze that made him blink and squint. Daylight? Then time had passed . . .

A small, flying object came slanting down into the shaft from above. He raised himself a little to see, and as he did so, the object hit the upper wall of the shaft and exploded. The sound of the explosion reverberated horribly in the great well. This was the thunder he had heard, and now that he was awake it threatened to crack his eardrums. Small bits of metal whizzed close by him.

"Chane!"

It was the voice of John Dilullo. It sounded frantic, and a long way off.

"Chane—get up!"

Chane turned his head drunkenly and saw Dilullo. He was not a long way off at all. He was standing right at the edge of the grid, on the metal walkway over the abyss.

Chane said, quite sensibly he thought, "You shouldn't stand there, John. You'll get hit."

Dilullo leaned toward him, dangerously close. "Get off that grid! You hear me, Chane? *Get off the grid.*" He shook his head impatiently and swore, and shouted louder. "McGoun says if you stay there much longer the Free-Faring force will start the cycle all over again. Get up. Come here to me."

Chane looked around. Vreya still lay there unmoving. So did Ashton and Raul and Sattargh. She had not yet been able to find them, then, to coax them back . . .

"You want to go out there again, Chane? Has it got you, too—like these others you were so busy sneering at?"

"No," said Chane. "Oh, hell, no! Not again."

He got onto his hands and knees and began moving. Presently he was on his feet, and then he was on the walkway with Dilullo's arm holding him as he staggered.

Another crash of thunder went off overhead.

"What . . . ?" mumbled Chane.

"Helmer's three planes," said Dilullo. "They can't go right over the shaft but they're firing missiles into it from a little distance. Trying to destroy the Free-Faring—and us."

Chane looked all around, and then up. He could not see even a mark on the shining metal walls up there.

"No damage yet," said Dilullo, still supporting and guiding him as they went along the walkway. "We've taken shelter in the tunnel. But sooner or later, the missile fragments will hit those people on the grid."

"She's bringing them," Chane said. "Vreya. At least, I think she is."

They reached the mouth of the tunnel. Inside, McGoun and Garcia and the three other Mercs were sitting. Chane sat down and leaned his back against the wall, and they looked at him in a strange way, almost in awe.

"What was it like?" asked Bollard.

"Oh," said Chane. "You believe it now."

"I guess I have to. What did it feel like."

Chane shook his head. He didn't answer for a moment. Then he said, "When I was a little boy, my father used to tell me about heaven. I didn't like the sound of it. The beauty and the glory part of it were all right, but the rest of it, the not having any physical being and the sitting around doing nothing except to feel holy—that seemed awfully useless. It wouldn't be *you*. Not really."

He paused, then said, "Out there, it was something like that kind of heaven."

He looked back at the distant grid, shimmering in the sunlight. None of the four figures on it had stirred.

There was another burst of thunder high in the well, and a second one followed it almost instantly.

"From the way those bursts come," said Bollard, "Helmer must be using all three of his planes."

McGoun caught at that. "Then why don't we get out through the tunnel and get away while they're busy up there?"

"Because," said Dilullo, "we haven't got what we came for. We haven't got Ashton."

"But don't you realize," pleaded McGoun, "that Helmer will never let any of us get away from here alive?"

"I realize it," said Dilullo. "But we don't go yet."

"Then I'll go by myself," raged McGoun. "The hell with Ashton. I'm going!"

"Go right ahead," said Dilullo. "I'd be glad to be rid of your babblings. But I have to warn you that Helmer has undoubtedly left a couple of men to blast anybody who comes out of the tunnel."

McGoun sat down again, and was silent.

"I *think* somebody out on that thing stirred a little," said Bollard, staring out at the grid.

"Come on, then," said Dilullo. "Not you, Chane—stay here and get your strength back. I think you'll be needing it pretty soon."

Dilullo, Bollard, and Garcia ran out along the walkway. Chane looked after them. He did not feel particularly weak. But his brain seemed a little numb, and would not quite clear.

Dilullo and the other two stood just outside the grid now, making beckoning motions. They blocked vision. It was not until they turned around, supporting two people, that Chane could see who had awakened.

Raul and Ashton.

Both men seemed so weak and nerveless that Dilullo and the others had to half carry them along the walkway and the ledge and into the tunnel. There they set them down, exhausted by even that small effort.

Ashton stared around him in a dazed, unseeing fashion. He seemed perplexed by the unfamiliar faces.

"Who . . . ?" he started to say, and stopped and shook his head, and began again. "Someone told me . . . if I didn't come back, the Free-Faring would be destroyed. Who . . . ?"

He ran out of breath again. Chane looked at him and thought that Bollard had been right, and this Randall Ashton they had come so far to find was not worth the effort. He looked a bit like his brother, only darker, younger, more handsome. But the good looks were spoiled by a petulant weakness in his expression.

Just now the weakness was physical as well. He was thin and wasted as though by a long illness. Chane thought that if this was what the delights of the Free-Faring made of a man, the thing was no damned good.

Raul spoke now, for the first time. "Vreya?" He too was looking at these strangers, puzzled, confused. Once, Chane could see, he had been as fine a physical specimen as

Helmer, but now his tall frame had fallen away to bone and ropy muscle, and his great blond head drooped as though his neck no longer had the strength to support it. "Vreya," he said again. "Vreya!"

"So she found you," Chane said. "But she hasn't come back herself."

Ashton said, "Who are you? And where is . . ." He was making an effort to collect his wits. Underneath the confusion was a growing anger. "Helmer, Vreya said. Helmer would destroy the Free-Faring. So I came back. That girl made me come back!" He started to get up. "Is it true, or was that just a lie, to get me . . ."

He lost his balance and Dilullo caught him, eased him down again.

"It's no lie, Mr. Ashton. Just sit quiet there, and I'll . . ."

But Ashton's eyes had cleared suddenly. He was looking at Dilullo, and the anger was now full grown and ugly.

"You're Mercs," he said. "Who hired you to come here?"

"Your brother, Mr. Ashton."

"My brother. My goddamned meddling brother. Wants me back, I suppose, for my own good." The anger in his face grew hotter. He began to tremble. "I will not leave this place. Not for my brother, not for anybody. Do you understand?"

Raul whispered Vreya's name again, and Chane followed his gaze to the grid. He thought—

Before Dilullo could prevent him, he ran out and across the walkway to the grid.

Vreya still lay motionless, her splendid golden body sprawled near the edge of the grid. Beyond her lay the Arcturian scientist, Sattargh. He had the faint red skin and aquiline face of his kind, and he made not the slightest movement either.

Two missiles *blam-blammed* almost together against the wall of the shaft high above, and fragments rattled off the walkway.

Chane squatted down on the walkway, only two feet away from Vreya, staring at her still form.

Another missile went off above, and this time a fragment ricocheted off the grid only inches away from Sattargh. The glasslike grid and the metal walkways seemed as impervious as the walls.

"Chane, come back here!"

That was Dilullo, with his commander's voice, but Chane paid no attention to the call. He waited, while the missiles went off above. He watched Vreya.

He thought he saw a slight movement of her fingers. She might be back, but still unconscious, numbed, as he had been.

Chane leaned forward, as far as he dared. "Vreya!" he said loudly. "Wake up. Get up."

There was no sign that she heard, no more movements. Chane made his voice harsher, louder.

"Vreya! Wake up or I'll whip you!"

It seemed to take a little time for that to penetrate, but presently she opened her eyes. They were bemused, dazed, but also they had a spark of anger in them.

"Up, I say, or I'll give you the best whipping you ever had in your life!"

He glared at her, and she glared back, her eyes focusing more steadily, the color rising in her cheeks. He lifted his hand, and she made a furious small sound and got to her feet and lurched toward him, her own hand raised to strike.

The moment she came off the grid Chane grabbed her. He held her, easily now because her strength had not returned yet, and he laughed and said in her ear, "Forgive me, Vreya, but you're such a damn strong-willed wench that I thought only a threat like that would get you up."

He picked her up in his arms and carried her back across the walkway and to the tunnel. He set her down carefully, and she sat limply and gave him a stormy look.

It was nothing to the look Ashton was giving Dilullo. He

appeared like a man on the verge of losing his mind. But he was not saying anything. Not for the moment. And Dilullo's mouth was set like a steel trap.

Presently Sattargh stirred feebly on the grid, and Bollard and Dilullo ran out and got him and brought him back.

"Thanks, Vreya," said Chane. "Thanks for getting them back here."

"Now that they are back," said Dilullo, "we can try getting the hell out of here. We'll never have a better chance than now, when most of them are up in those fliers."

Vreya said, "I thought you were going to fight Helmer, to save the Free-Faring. Did you lie to me, Chane?"

"Of course he lied," said Ashton. "They don't give a damn about the Free-Faring. All they care about is taking me away from it."

Chane noticed that Dilullo and Bollard were standing between Ashton and the mouth of the tunnel, as though they thought he might try to break back to the grid, missiles and all. Chane took the hint and kept a close eye on Vreya. She was sitting beside Raul now, her hand on his.

Chane said, "We can't fight very effectively from this tunnel, can we?"

She watched him, unconvinced. Raul sat with his head leaned back against the wall, and he watched Vreya, except for the times when he would lift his free hand and look at it, and touch his face, and then his body, feeling the gaunt bones. Chane thought, *He loves her. Perhaps he's thinking now what he almost lost in the Free-Faring.*

He wondered if she loved him. And was astonished at the twinge of jealousy he felt.

The Mercs were collecting their gear while Dilullo brooded.

McGoun said nastily, "You told me the entrance to the tunnel would be guarded."

Dilullo looked at him. "It will be, for sure. Which means

we'll have to fight our way out. But if we can do it, and get to the skitter-flier, we have a chance."

He turned to Milner. "You're the best with a laser. Chane, you're the fastest. You two, I think."

Neither made any objection. Milner said, "A light-bomb would help us."

Dilullo nodded. "I thought of that." He took from a pocket a little plastic sphere no bigger than a marble and handed it to Milner. Then he said, "I don't like killing, everybody knows that. But these fanatics intend to kill every one of us, so—take no chances."

Chane still had no boots on. While Milner removed his, Vreya said,

"You did lie."

"About the need to come back, no. About saving the Free-Faring . . ." Chane shrugged. "So far Helmer hasn't done it much damage."

Raul spoke suddenly, with startling violence. "He must. He must destroy it."

Vreya stared at him, shocked. "You can say that, Raul? After you've done it?"

"Because I have done it," he said. "Yes. Look at me, look at Ashton and Sattargh. The Free-Faring is sweet poison, but that is what it is. It is death."

Milner said, "Be sure to bring our boots." Bollard nodded. Milner turned to Chane. They took their lasers and started down the tunnel.

They went quite noiselessly; it was perfectly silent except for the echo from the great shaft behind them when missiles went off. It was dark here in the tunnel, but they could not lose their way.

After a while there was glimmer from up ahead. They went more softly until they were near the bright daylight of the tunnel end.

Milner held up his hand, signalling Chane to stop. Then

he drew the little sphere from his pocket, touched a stud on it, and hurled it out through the tunnel opening.

Instantly, Milner and Chane shut their eyes and clapped their free hands over their eyelids.

They knew when the light-bomb went off, not only by the sharp snapping sound that was intended to signal its detonation, but also by the fact that the blaze of light it created was so terrifically intense that even through hand and eyelid it registered.

Next moment, they opened their eyes and plunged out of the tunnel. Chane was first, going low and going fast, not caring if Milner saw his Starwolf speed, in this moment of utter danger.

His speed saved him. For an instant later, the laser mounted in a fixed stand on the ledge to cover the tunnel-mouth was triggered off by an Arkuun man whose eyes were still utterly dazzled.

The laser cut Milner almost in half. Chane bounded to one side as Milner fell.

There were two of the Arkuuns left here to guard the tunnelmouth, and their eyes were beginning to recover and they could see well enough now to kill. They swung their lasers toward Chane.

Chane shot one down, leaping aside with all his blurring Varnan speed just after the weapon's flash and crack.

The remaining Arkuun shot and missed, and then tried to swing his weapon to follow Chane. But already Chane, his teeth showing in a mirthless grin, was firing. The second Arkuun went down.

Chane bent over Milner. There was no doubt at all that he was dead.

Chane ran into the tunnel and put all the power of his lungs into a shout that echoed and re-echoed down the long tube.

"Come on!"

Presently he heard them coming. When they got to him,

Dilullo looked down at Milner and said nothing. He just dropped the boots that Milner would no longer need.

As Chane put on his own boots, the others arrived. Bollard and Janssen were dragging Ashton between them.

"I won't go," Ashton was saying, over and over. "I will not leave the Free-Faring!"

Dilullo turned on him and said, "We took a contract to bring you home, Mr. Ashton, and we'll keep it. There's nothing in the contract that says I can't encourage you to come quietly, so here's some encouragement."

And he gave Ashton a violent crack across the mouth with the back of his hard hand.

"Bring him," he said. "And bring Milner's body."

XVII

THEY WENT OUT OF the tunnel and along the ledge. Dilullo kept them hugging the inward side.

"Those fliers are still circling around up there over the summit," he said. "If we're spotted going down the mountain, it'll be bad."

When they had followed the ancient path down off the ledge and onto the rock-strewn slope, Dilullo halted them in the concealment of a big boulder. He nodded to Janssen and Bollard, who had carried Milner's body with them.

"This is far enough," he said. "We'll build a cairn over him. But don't show yourselves."

"This is insane," said McGoun, looking upward at the sky, a badly frightened man. "The man's dead, and—"

Dilullo interrupted. "Yes, the man's dead, and he wasn't the man I liked best in the world. But he was a good Merc and he followed me here to die. He's going to have a proper burial."

In the shadow of the big boulder, they built the cairn over Milner's body.

"All right," said Dilullo. "We're starting down now, but not all together. We'll move one or two at a time, from one bit of cover to the next. I'll lead, and you follow the way I go. Bollard, you can help Ashton. Chane, bring up the rear."

They moved out, Dilullo scuttering fast to another big boulder a little way down the slope, then Bollard following with Ashton. Chane thought that Ashton did actually need a helping hand, but that the real reason Dilullo had Bollard stick with him was to make sure he didn't desert them and go back up to the tunnel. Ashton was talking in a moaning whimper now about the Free-Faring, and how he could not leave it.

Chane, waiting to go last, glanced up at the three fliers circling the summit. Then he looked down at his own party, running by ones and twos from boulder to boulder, a deadly game of follow-the-leader.

Chane did not think they could long remain undiscovered. The Mercs were pretty good at this sort of thing, but Ashton and Sattargh and Garcia were not, and neither was Raul, nor Vreya.

They did not even get as far as Chane expected. They were barely a third of the way down the rocky slope when Chane, glancing upward again, saw one of the three fliers break off its circling of the summit and come rushing down toward them.

Chane yelled a warning and skipped behind a rock. He raised his laser, but the Arkuuns seemed to know the range of a portable and the flier kept well above it as the pilot let his missiles go.

The explosion filled the air with rock fragments. Chane peered, but his comrades were all hidden and he didn't know if any of them had been hit.

"Pinned!" he muttered to himself. "That about does it."

The flier went on out away from the mountain so it could circle and come back over them again.

Now the Arkuuns in the other two fliers up there had waked up to what was happening, and they came hurrying to join the attack.

Chane, watching, thought that one of the two, in its haste, went almost over the summit of the mountain. He hoped that the shaft of the Free-Faring had caught it.

His hope died when both fliers came straight on down

toward them. The missiles from the lead flier began to bang around him.

Chane hugged his rock. At the same time he glanced away from the mountain. The first of their attackers would be circling back and catch them on the wrong side of their shelters.

The last of the fliers came down over him. To his surprise, it fired no missiles at all. It just went majestically downward in a straight, declining line until it hit the slope and ploughed up the rocks and vanished in flaming wreckage.

"So the Free-Faring *did* catch that one!" thought Chane. "Good."

It did not much help his party, though. Pinned on the mountainside as they were, two fliers were quite enough to finish them off as long as the pilots stayed out of laser range.

The first flier had circled and now was coming back. Chane skipped to the other side of the builder; as he did so, he saw Dilullo and the others down there below doing the same thing. He thought a few of them were missing, but could not be sure.

The missiles exploded in a line up the slope. One went off close to the boulder behind which Chane crouched.

Chane jumped up and staggered out into the open. He clutched his middle with his free hand. Then he collapsed onto the ground, lying on his back with his eyes open, the laser still clutched in his hand.

To his amazement, as he lay there, he heard feet pounding up the path. Dilullo, sweating and with his chin bleeding from a small gash, looked down at him.

Chane?"

Chane did not move a muscle. He said, "Get the devil out of here, John, and leave me alone. And try to work your way farther down the slope."

"Ah, I might have known it was some Starwolf trick," Dilullo muttered, but all the same he looked relieved.

He pounded back down the slope. Then Chane heard one of the two fliers coming back toward the mountain, and heard its missiles banging again.

The flier circled around without loosing any missiles in Chane's vicinity. He began to hope.

It went on and on as he lay there, the fliers relentlessly coming toward the mountainside and firing, and then circling to swing out again. But the uproar seemed to be moving gradually down the slope. Dilullo would be trying to work them lower between attacks, Chane thought.

Lying still, with his arms outflung, he watched each time as the flier that had just attacked came circling over him. The fliers were getting closer to him, for though they stayed out of range of Dilullo and his party, the movement of the party down the slope was lowering the altitude of the attackers. And they had obviously ceased to worry about Chane.

Another banging of missiles and the flier came on and curved around over Chane, lower than before.

Not yet, he thought. *I've got to be sure . . .*

He waited and heard the attack still receding down the slope. He wondered how many of Dilullo's party still survived.

Then, when the sound was even more distant, Chane sensed that the moment had come, and gathered himself. He waited until the flier curved above him; this time it was low enough.

With all the speed that Varna had given him, he jumped up, aimed the laser and let go with it.

The bolt went right through the cockpit. The flier did not complete the curve it had begun. It rammed straight into the side of the mountain.

The remaining Arkuun flier, which had been circling around to come in for another attack-run, changed course.

The pilot seemed to have become crazed with rage, for he dived the flier straight at Chane, letting missiles go in a steady stream.

Chane had leaped to cover, but the rocks seemed to lift up around him and the air was full of dust. The explosions almost stunned him.

He staggered out when the explosions stopped, but the flier had already swung around and was winging out to turn and make another run at him.

Chane saw Dilullo, over a way from him on the slope, climbing higher than Chane's position, running like mad.

Then Chane ducked and once more the explosions were all around him and he thought when they stopped that he was stretching his luck pretty thin, that he would not get through another of these salvos.

But as the explosions stopped, he heard another sound—the crack of a laser. He jumped up, but he could see nothing for a moment, through the dust.

It cleared a little, and he saw the last Arkuun flier fluttering over and over. It hit the ground and rolled a little way down the slope.

Dilullo came limping down toward him, carrying his laser. "I am not," said Dilullo, "as cunning as a Starwolf at these tricks, but I can imitate them when I see them. I figured that pilot was so mad at you he wouldn't be looking for me higher up."

They went to the wrecked fliers and examined them. No one was alive in them. In one of them Helmer sat with his head lolled back. On his gold-skinned face was nothing now, just a dead-expression.

"Damn all fanatics," said Dilullo bitterly. "They get themselves and a lot of other people killed because they won't argue for their ideas—they have to enforce them."

Chane shrugged. "Well," he said carelessly, "he didn't destroy the Free-Faring, and he didn't destroy us. At least not all of us. How many are left?"

"Raul took a missile fragment right through the heart. McGoun got another fragment in the stomach, and I think he's bought it. Janssen has a shoulder wound, but not bad."

It was very quiet now on that upper slope. The wind blew through the broken cockpit of the flier and stirred Helmer's bright hair. Dilullo turned and walked wearily away, down toward where the others were. Chane followed him, feeling a little sorry for him and not envying him his conscience.

When they reached the others, Bollard was giving first aid to McGoun, who seemed to be unconscious. Vreya sat crying beside the body of Raul. The others seemed a little stupefied.

"They're all done for," Dilullo told them. "You're safe now. Stay here till you get McGoun tended to and then make a sling litter for him. Chane and I are going down to the skitter-flier."

They started away. When they had gone perhaps fifty yards there was a sudden outcry behind them. They turned, and saw Randall Ashton running away from the group, back up the mountain toward the tunnel-mouth.

Chane said, "I'll get him." He shouted to Bollard to stay where he was and take care of McGoun. Then he trotted after Ashton. There was no hurry about it. He watched Ashton pant and strain and stagger up the steep path, watched him stumble and fall and get up again. *Go on, you bastard,* he thought, *cry for it. Enough men have died because of you that you damn well ought to cry.*

And he was crying when Chane caught up to him, sitting in the dust with the tears running on his cheeks and the sobs choking him. Chane picked him and laid him across his shoulders, then took him down and dumped him onto the ground, where he lay exhausted.

Dilullo said, "Bollard, if he tries that again, knock him over with a stunner."

"I'd rather use a laser, but okay," said Bollard, not looking up from his work. He was almost as bloody as McGoun, working feverishly to stop a welling tide that would not be stopped. Chane was tempted to tell him that he was wasting his time, and then decided not to. It was Bollard's time, and anyway he would not welcome the Starwolf type of realism. These men always had to try. He went off again with Dilullo, and this time nothing stopped them.

All the way down the mountain Dilullo said not a word, but Chane knew what the other was thinking. He was thinking the same thing himself.

Highly unwelcome thoughts, but they turned out to be true. When they got into the nest of tall rocks where Janssen had hidden the skitter-flier, they found a fused and shattered wreck. Missiles had been fired carefully into it from close range.

"Helmer was a thorough man," said Dilullo. "Damn him."

"There's still Ashton's plane."

"Do you think he would have overlooked it?"

Chane shrugged.

"Well, we'll check it out. We'll get Ashton and . . ."

"Take a breather, John," said Chane. "I'll go and fetch him."

Dilullo looked at him bleakly. "I'm so old you want to spare me an extra trip up that slope, is that it?"

"You know," said Chane, "you ought to do something about that age-obsession of yours."

"Aren't Starwolves worried about getting old?" demanded Dilullo.

Chane grinned. "The kind of a life a Starwolf leads, he doesn't have too many worries on that score."

"Ah, get out of here and go," said Dilullo. "After all, why should I wear myself out when I've got a big dumb ox like you to run errands."

Chane went, fast, only slowing down when he came within sight of the others up on the slope.

"McGoun's gone," said Bollard. "Died before I could even get the bleeding all stopped."

Chane nodded. He looked at Vreya, who was not crying now but was sitting with her head drooping beside Raul's body.

"John would want you to build up some rocks over McGoun and Raul too, wouldn't he?" said Chane.

"I suppose he would," said Bollard.

Chane went to where Ashton was sitting. "Come along —we want you to show us where your flier's hidden."

"I will not," said Ashton. "I don't want to leave here. Why should I show you?"

A dark smile came onto Chane's face. "If you don't, I will do some things to you that will give me great pleasure."

Sattargh stood up. He said wearily, "I'll show you. I can't take any more of this."

The thin Arcturian went down the slope to where Dilullo was waiting. Then he led them for more than a mile along the base of the mountain.

"We couldn't hide it completely," he said, panting. "But we put sand and rock-dust over it wherever we could, to camouflage it."

When they reached the place to which Sattargh led them, a bay that indented the side of the mountain, they found what they expected to find. Ashton's flier was a fused and shapeless mess.

"Now what?" Chane asked Dilullo.

Dilullo said, "Give me a little time to think up a brilliant inspiration. While I'm doing it, you can tell the others to come on down here."

A few hours later, as Allubane was setting, they sat in a circle and ate their rations and looked dismally at each other. When they had finished eating, Dilullo spoke.

"Now I'll tell you how we stand," he said. "We have no flier to get us out of here. We have no long-range communicator, so we can't call Kimmel on Allubane Two and have him bring the ship here."

He got out the map and spread it out, and had Bollard shine his hand-lamp on it as the dusk gathered.

"Now, a Merc likes to have two strings to his bow," said Dilullo. "I plotted out a rendezvous with Kimmel. If he didn't hear from us at all, he was to come to that rendezvous every ten days."

He put his finger on the spot where the great river that flowed north-south ran into one of Arkuu's seas.

"That's where the rendezvous is," he said.

"And where are we?" asked Garcia.

Dilullo put his finger down on another spot on the map. "Here."

"That's an awful long way," said Garcia. "Hundreds of miles . . ."

"It is," said Dilullo. "But I've thought up a way we can get to that rendezvous."

"So you've thought up a brilliant inspiration after all?" said Chane.

"Yes, I have," answered Dilullo.

"What is it?" Chane asked. "How do we get there?"

Dilullo looked around at them and said,

"We walk."

XVIII

How LONG HAD THEY been walking? Chane tried to reckon it up in his mind. Fourteen days crossing the mountain ranges—no, sixteen, counting the two days they had lost in following a blind lead and returning from it. But how many days in the great forest? How many following the slope of the land downward until it grew hot and humid, and the great trees were replaced by this crimson jungle?

When they had first come over the mountains, Chane had objected to the course Dilullo set.

"This isn't a direct course to the rendezvous. You're angling away northward."

Dilullo had nodded. "But this is the shortest route to that big river."

"The river?"

"Chane, look at these people, the shape some of them are in. They'll never last out the distance to the rendezvous on foot. But if I can get them to the river, we can raft down it to the meeting place."

Chane, looking ahead along the line of his companions as they went through the red jungle, thought to himself that they may have looked poor then, but that that wasn't a patch on the way they looked now.

Sattargh was in the worst shape, but Ashton was not much better. The long periods they had spent in the Free-Faring, returning at only infrequent intervals for food, had sapped their stamina. Garcia was doing better, but he was a scholar, not an adventurer, and he tired fast.

Both Chane and Dilullo had worried about Vreya, but Chane thought now that they needn't have. The tall Arkuun girl was magnificent. Her fine golden legs strode along firmly, and she made no complaints about anything.

The yellow sunlight shafted down in broken bars through the dark red foliage of the taller trees. The smaller growth was a bright scarlet. They plodded along after Dilullo, whose turn it was to lead the way, and they had to stop now and then while Dilullo slashed away some impending brush.

Stopping thus now, Chane noticed that Sattargh and Ashton sat wearily down on the ground, even for this short halt. It was a bad sign. Sattargh was trying, but Ashton was sullen and resentful, and neither of them really had the strength for this trek.

It seemed very silent in the red jungle. Chane had noticed many birds, some of them surprisingly big and exotic looking, but he had seen very few animals.

He said so to Vreya, standing beside him and brushing her yellow hair back from her damp face, and she nodded.

"The Nanes have almost exterminated many species, except a few kinds of big carnivores in the far south."

Chane thought of the pretty little mouth of the thing he had struggled with. "I wouldn't have thought those things could be flesh-eaters. I saw no teeth."

"They were designed to take liquid artificial food," said Vreya. "But they learned to beat animal flesh into a pulp and ingest it that way."

"Nice," said Chane, and at that moment Dilullo finished cutting and they started forward again.

Chane looked narrowly at Sattargh and Ashton. Sattargh struggled to his feet, but Ashton looked as though he was just going to sit there. Then he looked up and saw Chane's eye upon him, and got up.

Chane thought, *At least two days yet, maybe more, and we'll have trouble with him long before that.*

That night they made camp under tall trees, where there

was no brush. They made no fire—there was no reason to ask for trouble. They chewed their super-nutritious food tablets and drank the water they had got from streams along the way sterilized with steritablets. As on each night so far, Dilullo insisted that Sattargh and Ashton eat more of the food than they wanted.

Chane sat on the edge of the little clearing, with his back against a big tree and his laser across his knees. Both moons were up and throwing beams of tarnished silver through the foliage. Presently Vreya came through the slanting silver bars of light, and sat down beside him. She uttered a sigh of weariness.

"You've been wonderful, Vreya," he told her. "I didn't think any woman could do it."

"I tire," she said. "But I have something to take back to my people, and I am going to do it."

"The Free-Faring? You'll tell them about it?"

"I will," she said. "I'll take them to it, as many as I can. I'll have them go out in the Free-Faring and see how glorious the outer stars and worlds can be. And we'll open the Closed Worlds, for all time to come."

"You'll only get caught by that insidious thing, the way Ashton and Sattargh and Raul were caught," he said. "You'll end up as they would have ended if we hadn't come."

She shook her head. "No. I will not be caught. *You* were not caught, because you have some wild strength in you that I cannot understand. I too have strength."

"What about those who don't have it?"

"I've thought of that. We'll find some way to protect them, make sure they don't go too far. It can be done, Chane. It's a risk, yes. But what is ever gained without risk?"

He couldn't answer that. Least of all, he.

On the following morning, two hours after they started, Sattargh collapsed. His legs simply crumpled under him.

"Just a little rest," he panted. "I'll be all right then . . ."

Chane had come to have an admiration for the thin, aging Arcturian scholar. He said, "All right, get a rest. I'll tell John."

Dilullo came back, his long face getting longer as he looked at Sattargh.

"Ten minutes rest," said Sattargh. "Then I can go on."

But when the ten minutes had passed and he tried to get up, he fell back.

"Ah-huh," said Dilullo. "I thought so. Get out the sling litter."

The litter, a compact net of thin, strong strings, was affixed to two poles cut from the brush. Garcia took the front end of it and Chane the rear, and they went on.

By the time they camped that night, they were an exhausted lot, except for Chane. They sprawled on the ground in the darkness, unable even to eat until they had some rest. Chane sat, chewing his food-tablets.

Something lithe and white and swift flashed out of the darkness and snatched up Ashton's limp form from the edge of the group and darted away with it.

In a split-second Chane was on his feet and hurling himself in pursuit. He used all his Starwolf speed, not caring whether the others saw or not.

He was only a few yards behind the Nane. The creature could probably have distanced him if it had been unburdened, but it would not let go of Ashton. Crashing through brush, leaping fallen logs, Chane put on a terrific burst of speed. They had come a long way for Ashton, and gone through a lot, and Ashton himself might not be worth it, but the work and wounds and death were not going to be for nothing.

The Nane dropped Ashton and tore with unbelievable strength at Chane's arms. Chane locked his hands together like iron and yelled.

"John! Here!"

The Nane made mewing, sobbing sounds, and struggled

146

to break Chane's grip. Chane did not think he could hold it many moments longer.

There was a crashing in the brush and Dilullo and Bollard came running through the broken moonlight. They had their jungle knives, and they stabbed them into the Nane's body.

The Nane stopped trying to break Chane's grip, and struck with its hands, and Dilullo went flying backward.

Bollard stabbed again and again. Chane could hear the knifeblade driving home with a strange dull sound, as though it was sticking into some sort of sponge.

"Can't *kill* the thing," Bollard panted.

Chane suddenly let go of the Nane's neck. Still riding the creature's back, he shifted his grip downward to pinion the thing's arms.

The strength of those arms was so great that Chane knew he could not hold the grip more than a few seconds. Bollard hacked and stabbed furiously, and all at once the Nane fell down and lay still.

"My God, what a thing," said Bollard, gasping. He was utterly shaken. "Didn't seem to have any vital organs at all . . ."

Chane ran to where Dilullo was getting up from the tangle of brush into which the Nane had hurled him.

"No bones broken," said Dilullo, "but I'll have some bruises. When the critter grabbed me to throw me, I thought its hands would break me in half."

Bollard was bending over Ashton's limp form.

"Choked unconscious," he said. "Probably to keep him from crying out when the thing grabbed him. He should come round."

They carried Ashton back into camp. "Three men on guard at all times," said Dilullo. "Each with one of the lasers."

Vreya was looking at Chane in wonder. "You pursued a Nane?" she said. "I didn't think anyone . . ."

"Looks like we're getting back into their territory," said Dilullo.

Vreya nodded. "Yes, the dead city M'lann where most of the Nanes were created long ago is not too far southeast of here."

Dilullo got out his map and a hand-lamp, and squatted on the ground studying. "Yes," he said. "M'lann's about a hundred and fifty miles southeast. The river runs through it."

He snapped off the light. "All right, those not on guard might as well get some sleep. We need rest bad enough."

Next morning, they found that the nightmare attack had had one beneficent result. Randall Ashton had recovered consciousness in a state of absolute horror. He made none of his usual sullen objections when they started. He kept looking nervously around the jungle and then back at his companions, as though he was afraid they might leave him alone here. Sattargh said that this day he was able to walk.

In mid-afternoon, as they went along the bank of a small stream. Chane saw a white shape flitting in the brush and let go with his laser at it.

Ten minutes later, two Nanes flashed from behind big trees just ahead of them. Dilullo fired and missed, but Bollard, who had the third laser, cut one down and the other flashed away.

"The woods seem to be full of them," said Bollard. "Have they got some way of letting each other know we're here?"

Chane wondered about that too. The very fact of the existence of the Nanes was nightmarish. They were a by-product of that same science that had produced the Free-Faring, and Chane thought that that science had been a curse to this world, creating a horde of almost immortal horrors to prey upon all life.

That night, Dilullo was sitting rubbing his bruises when Chane gave up his guard post to Janssen. Dilullo said nothing for a time, but his face had deep lines of pain and fatigue etched into it.

"I was just thinking," he said finally. "I was thinking of a beautiful white house, with a fountain and flowers and everything in it the finest. I was wondering if it's worth it."

Chane grinned. "You'll have your fine house someday, John. And you'll sit in front of it and admire your flowers for two weeks, and then you'll get up and go back to Merc Hall."

Dilullo looked at him. "That's what I like about you, Chane—you're always so cheery and encouraging. Will you please get away from me?"

Twice in the night they were awakened by laser blasts, as their guards fired at lurking Nanes. In the morning they learned that one of the lasers was dead, its charge exhausted.

Dilullo nodded. "I'm not surprised; we used them pretty freely on Helmer's fliers. Save the other two as much as you can."

That day's march was as nightmarish as the one before, with only one actual attempted attack by Nanes, but with frequent sight of one or two of the creatures slipping along parallel with them.

They had to carry Sattargh most of that day. And by night, Chane saw that Randall Ashton was giving out. He was trying hard; he had been so frightened that he dreaded the possibility of being left behind. But he was just not going to make it much further.

Vreya lay that night as in a stupor when Chane went to her, her eyes closed, her breath gasping. Yet she still had not made one complaint.

He stroked her hair. Weakly, she took his hand to her mouth and made to bite his finger.

Chane laughed and hugged her. "Vreya, I've never seen a girl like you."

"Go away and let me sleep," she mumbled.

Ashton began to give out before they had gone an hour on the next day's march. He started to fall over small obstacles. When Chane was not helping to carry the litter, he took Ashton's shoulder and steadied him.

"Thanks," said Ashton. "I . . . I don't want to fall behind . . ."

Dilullo suddenly called a halt. Ahead of them the tall trees thinned out and they glimpsed a wide tawny flood, turned to brilliance by the yellow light of Allubane.

The river.

They sat down on its bank and for a while they were too stupid and exhausted to do anything but just look at it, the vast heaving flood, rolling between jungled banks, coming out of mystery above, going into mystery below.

"All right," said Dilullo finally. "A raft won't build itself. We haven't got tools to cut trees so we'll have to use one of the lasers. Bollard, see to it. I'll stand guard with the other laser."

The scorching lash of the laser felled and trimmed the trees they needed. But by the time they finished, that laser was exhausted also.

Chane rolled the logs down to the river. Bollard brought from one of the packs a coil of steeltwine, thin as cord and strong as cable.

As he showed Chane how to bind the logs together, Bollard said, "I used to read stories where they would bind logs together with vines and make rafts. Did you ever see a vine that would tie anything together so it'd stay tied?"

"I've been on a lot of worlds, and I never did," said Chane.

They used the jungle knives to carve a steering-sweep and a yoke to set it in. Oddly, in all this time there was not a sign of the Nanes.

The raft floated readily. "All right, get our invalids aboard," said Dilullo.

The exhausted members of the party stumbled onto the

rough raft and promptly lay down. Chane pushed out into the current of the river with the long steering oar.

They floated. They went down and down the great river of Arkuu, and the sun set and the stars and moons came up, and then the yellow flare of Allubane rose into the sky again. Most of them just lay flat and rested. But on the first day on the raft, Vreya dived off it and swam around and around, and then got back on board and lay down to dry herself and her short jerkin in the sun.

Chane gave her a leering wink as she lay there. She stuck out her tongue at him and he broke up laughing.

They went down the river and there seemed nothing at all to see but the jungle-covered banks. On the third night, Chane sat with Dilullo at the steering sweep while the others slept. Both moons were in the zenith, and the river had become a running sea of silver.

"Faster than light across the stars," said Dilullo. "And then ten miles an hour on a raft. I feel like an aging Huckleberry Finn."

"Who is Huckleberry Finn?" asked Chane.

"You know, Chane, I'm sorry for you," said Dilullo. "You're an Earthman by descent, but you've got no frame of reference. You don't know the legends, the myths, the stories . . ."

"We have some good legends on Varna," said Chane.

"I'll just bet," said Dilullo. "How Harold Hardhand the Starwolf went raiding and broke a lot of skulls and stole a lot of other people's goods and came home triumphant."

"Something like that," Chane admitted, and then he suddenly got to his feet, staring intently ahead.

The moonlit river was sweeping around in a great curve, and ahead of them on both sides of the river there loomed great, dark ruined towers against the moonlit sky.

"That," said Dilullo, "would be the dead city M'lann."

Chane nodded. "Yes. And look what's waiting for us there."

XIX

AT FIRST GLANCE, it looked as though the moonlit ruined city was crowded with hordes of Nanes. Then Chane realized that actually the creatures could be counted only in the dozens, but as he had never seen so many together before, they looked like a crowd. Their bodies gleaming white in the moonlight; they looked almost beautiful from this distance as they ran along the stone quays of the dead city, toward two massive half-ruined bridges.

"Wake up the others," said Dilullo. "We've got trouble."

Chane woke them, and they stared in fear and repulsion at the lithe white shapes. The raft was bearing them steadily down toward the first of the two bridges.

"We've got one laser still operative," said Dilullo. "We've got the ato-flashes—they won't last long, but get them out. There's also the jungle knives."

He added, "Chane, you take the sweep and steer. If we run aground, we're done for. Ashton, you and Sattargh don't have strength enough to do anything; I want you to lie down and hang on."

Chane went to the steering-sweep, and as he went he grabbed Vreya's arm and hustled her along, sitting her down behind the place where he stood at the sweep.

She opened her mouth to protest angrily, and then shut it. They were nearing the first bridge.

There were now at least fifteen Nanes on the bridge, looking in the moonlight like white ghost-men as they waited for the raft. From far across the towering ruins there came long, falling, wordless cries, an unhuman ululation that grew louder as other Nanes answered the calls.

"They're going to jump down on us, John," said Bollard.

"Close your eyes, everybody," said Dilullo, and hurled up three of the tiny light-bombs in quick succession.

Through closed eyelids, it was as though brilliant lightning flashed three times.

There were sounds of splashes nearby, and thumps of things hitting the raft. Chane opened his eyes to see that, even though momentarily blinded, the Nanes had jumped. There were two of them on the raft.

The laser cracked as Dilullo fired, and one of the two creatures on the raft fell overboard, scorched and lifeless. But the other one that had struck the raft had hit Garcia, and had now grabbed him; he was screaming.

Bollard and Janssen sprang upon the back of that Nane, plunging the jungle knives into its body, trying to do it to death and not succeeding. The creature dropped Garcia and whirled around, and at that moment Dilullo triggered the laser and killed it.

"They are coming from behind us," rang Vreya's voice from behind Chane.

The Nanes swam like white man-fishes, and from behind and on either side they were starting to leap up out of the water onto the raft.

Dilullo triggered, but the laser had gone dead. "Lie flat!" yelled Chane, and pulled the big steering-sweep out of its yoke and used all his strength to use it as a flail.

The old battle-cry that he and his comrades had used on so many worlds sprang from his lips. *"Kill, Starwolf!"* he yelled in the Varnan tongue, and swung his oar.

He knocked Nanes back into the water in two tremendous sweeps of the oar. Another of the things came up mewing onto the logs behind him, and Chane used the butt of the oar as a punch and drove the creature's face in.

"Steer!" yelled Dilullo. "Or we'll have more of them on us!"

Chane's battle-fury faded enough for him to see what Dilullo meant. They were drifting down toward the second bridge now. This one had a big section gone out of its central span, but on the projecting parts of it still intact, other Nanes were waiting. And they were going to drift under one of those ends.

Chane put the sweep back in its yoke and strained mightily. The raft swung lumberingly toward the center of the river.

Garcia was lying and moaning but nobody was paying any attention to him. White hands with nailless fingers came up out of the water and gripped the edge of the raft. Bollard spurted the little flare of his ato-flash at the hands, and they let go.

And amazingly, of a sudden, the fight was over. The raft went past the bridge and the creatures on its projecting broken ends seemed to realize they were too far away to reach the raft by swimming. They mewled and sobbed their wordless cries, but that was all.

"Well," said Dilullo. In the moonlight, his face was sweat-streaked and a little wild. "Let's see how we stand."

Garcia's both arms and some of his ribs had been broken by the grip of the Nane. Bollard's left wrist had been fractured by a blow. The others had only bruises.

"When I think how strong those things are, I wonder we're still alive," panted Dilullo. "You did damned good work with that sweep, Chane."

"You take it and steer," said Chane. "I'll help fix up Garcia and Bollard."

"I'll keep well away from shore," said Dilullo. "The last thing we need, if we're ever to get to that rendezvous, is more fighting."

XX

"You look," said Kimmel, "as though you've been having quite a time. Where's Milner?"

"He got it," said Dilullo.

They had waited five days at the rendezvous, where the great river ran into the heaving ocher-colored ocean, before the ship came and saw their smoke signal, and landed at the place which Dilullo had selected.

"You found the man?" asked Kimmel.

Dilullo waved his hand toward Ashton. "Mr. Randall Ashton."

"Found me? They kidnapped me," said Ashton. "I was all right, till they came . . ."

"You were lying there, slowly dying," said Dilullo. "You're going back with me, and I'll take you by the hand right into your brother's office and collect our wages for bringing you. But after that, if you want to come back here and do it all over again and kill yourself, that's perfectly all right with me."

Vreya looked at Chane, where they stood on the edge of the group.

"What about you, Chane? Will you come back some day and go Free-Faring with me again?"

"No," he said. "The Free-Faring is not for me. But maybe I'll come back, at that."

She shrugged her golden shoulders. "By then, I may have another man."

"That's all right," said Chane. "I'll just knock him out of the way."

Vreya smiled. "It sounds interesting."

Dilullo was giving Kimmel some instructions, and Kimmel looked as though he didn't like them.

"It's simple," said Dilullo. "Take the ship up to medium altitude and then come back down and land out on the clear land around that city Yarr. Vreya can get out and we can be on our way before they spot us."

"Now wait a moment," said Kimmel. "I don't like to run a chance going as close to the city as that. The ship . . ."

Dilullo surprised them all. An angry color came into his cheeks and his voice snapped.

"This girl is worth twenty ships," he said. "She has some cockeyed notions, but she acted like a soldier all the way. We'll do it the way I say, and set her down safe."

Vreya went and kissed him. Dilullo gave her an embarrassed smile, and patted her awkwardly on the shoulder.

They did it that way, at dusk, and the last Chane saw of Vreya was as she walked with her swinging stride toward the lights of Yarr.

They went back up fast into the glare of Allubane, and while Kimmel cautioned and pleaded with the imperturbable Mattock, Chane looked back at the Closed Worlds.

He did not think they would be closed much longer. He thought that Vreya had the strength to be a leader. And he thought now that she had been right when she said she was strong enough to resist the deadly lure of addiction to the Free-Faring.

Later, when they had gone into overdrive, Dilullo called him into his little cabin. He pushed the bottle toward him.

"Everybody who does good work likes to have it noticed," said Dilullo. "So I'll say now, you did good work, Chane. There were a couple of times when, without your strength and quickness, we wouldn't have pulled through."

"I thought so, too," said Chane.

Dilullo made a disgusted sound. "Ah, you just can't be nice to some people."

He poured himself another drink. Then he said,

"You know, Chane, you never did tell us much about what you did in the Free-Faring."

"No, I didn't," said Chane.

"Did you go to Varna?"

Chane nodded.

"I thought so," said Dilullo. "There was a kind of a homesick look on your face afterwards. Well, I'll tell you . . . there's different kinds of homesickness, and I've got a special kind of my own. So I think I know a little how you feel." Chane said, "I'm going to go back to Varna, sometime."

Dilullo looked at him, and then nodded his head.

"Chane, I think you will."

AN EPIC NEW SERIES OF GALACTIC ADVENTURE!

Edmond Hamilton's
STARWOLF!

ANOTHER GREAT SCIENCE FICTION ADVENTURE SERIES!

PROFESSOR JAMESON SPACE ADVENTURES!

F-420 — 40¢
PROFESSOR JAMESON #1:

The Planet of the Double Sun
by Neil R. Jones

With his cosmos-exploring comrades, Professor Jameson faces the strange enigma of the triped-creatures of THE PLANET OF THE DOUBLE SUN.

G-631 — 50¢
PROFESSOR JAMESON #2:

The Sunless World
by Neil R. Jones

Exploring deep inside a new planet, the Zoromes suddenly discover that this world is going to crash into another planet— and there is no time for escape!

G-650 — 50¢
PROFESSOR JAMESON #3:

Space War
by Neil R. Jones

Professor Jameson and the metal-encased Zorome machine men were not affected by ordinary perils—until they encountered the metal eaters of Mumed!

G-681 — 50¢
PROFESSOR JAMESON #4:

Twin Worlds
by Neil R. Jones

In the double-world system of Dlasitap, the Zoromes fight to free one planet from the tyranny of another.
